Animythical Tales

Animythical Tales

by Sarah Totton

FANTASTIC
BOOKS

Cover art from *The Bestiarium* by Aloys Zötl.

Editor: Douglas Cohen.

Fantastic Books
1380 East 17 Street, Suite 2233
Brooklyn, New York 11230
www.FantasticBooks.biz

ISBN: 978-1-5154-5817-3

Second Edition, 2024

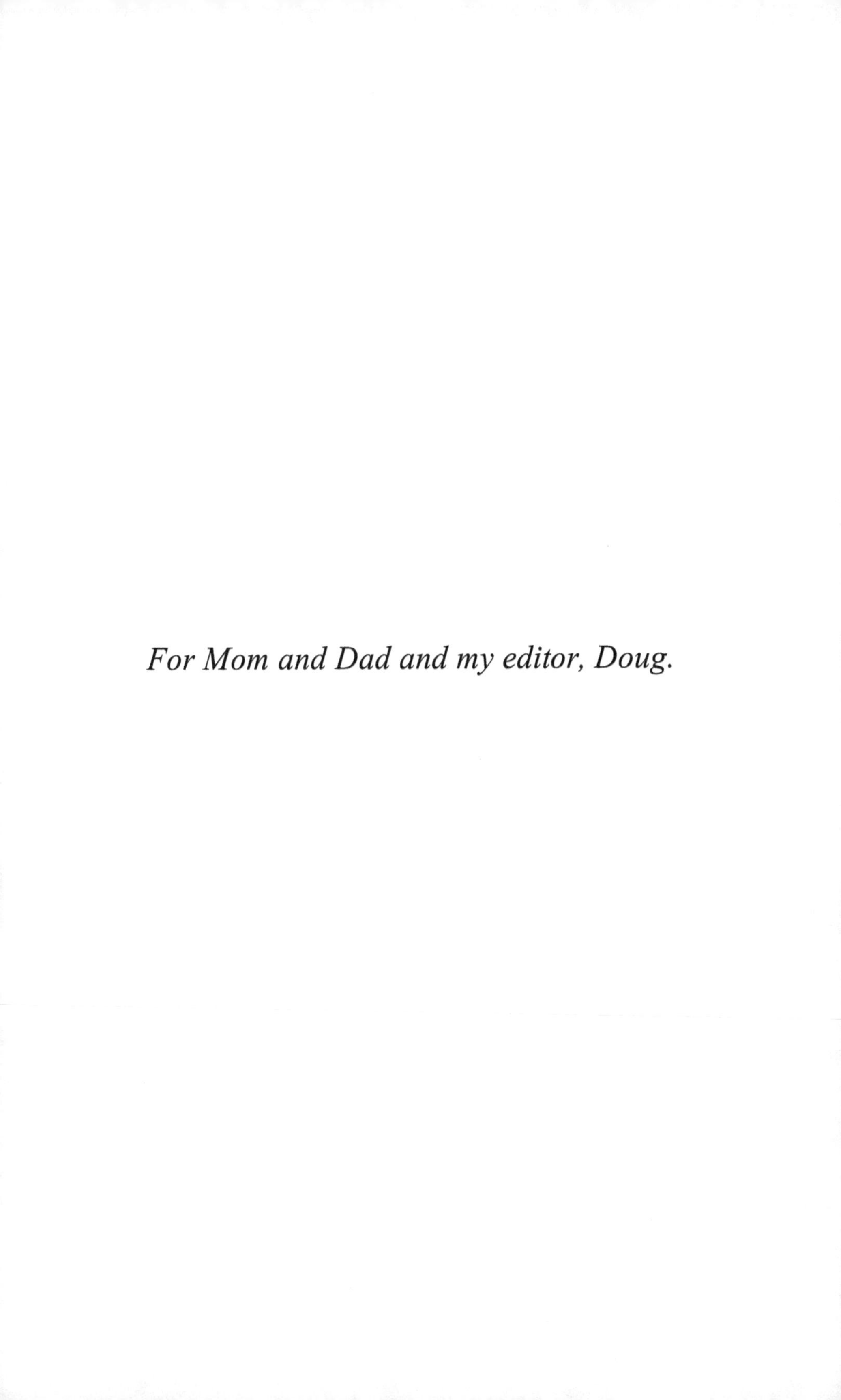

For Mom and Dad and my editor, Doug.

CONTENTS

Introduction
by Forrest Aguirre

Let's face cold, hard facts. Not many people make it through a busy editor's slush pile. I'll forego the statistics, but suffice it to say that the odds of an unsolicited submission making it through the first round of editorial cuts, while not astronomical, are fairly slim.

Occasionally, though, through gloomy nights of bleary-eyed reading, the editor spots a shimmer in the dark and looks more closely. Something shiny catches his attention, grabs him by the collar, and screams "You must look more closely!" The editor, wiping the rheum from his eyes, looks at this shiny thing and sees pleasing patterns emerge from the ink. Turns of phrase; quirky, lovable characters; enveloping settings. All of these combine and enwrap the editor, pulling him into the fictional world, only letting him come up for air long enough to say "I must show the world this beautiful thing I've found."

Sometimes that shine is just that—a false beauty, fish bait. Other times, when the shine is more closely examined, one begins to see the colors underlying the shine, the chromatic elements that give the shine its surface sparkle.

This is where Totton's work first grabbed my attention, in the "color" of her work. I don't know where there is any intentional symbolic purpose in Totton's use of color, that is a question best left answered by the author. But I have felt, at times, when reading her stories, like I'm walking into a field of Technicolor gems. Even in the grayest portions of her stories, one notices the lack of color first and foremost, like an Odilon Redon painting that has been drained of its hues by some demented anti-artistic vampire. There is a sense of loss in those word-landscapes that show just enough brightness to portray what might have been vis-à-vis the grayness of what is.

Beyond the mere descriptive, Totton's emotive pallet is a bit more complex. Gone are the rainbow colors, the distinctive, sharp visual lines that make her word-paintings so striking. This is not to say that her characterizations are muddled. Far from it. They just show a wide breadth of emotion. One cannot easily categorize Totton's characters because they are moving targets, capable of change and growth. These are not the melodramatic manic-depressives that so often infiltrate the realms of speculative fiction. These characters rarely brood or have unwarranted "happy attacks," put there for the sake of moving plot or establishing mood. They are more real, more like "the rest of us". Sometimes happy, sometimes sad, not omniscient, but not ignorant, not insatiably curious at all times, nor buried in ennui. Her characters dodge stereotypes, engaging the reader with their complex inner lives.

And this is where the reader (and the editor) become fully entrapped. Totton excels at luring her readers into her characters' labyrinthine hearts and minds. Once inside, for all their variation, the reader sees one repeated theme, whether implied or explicit, that seems to provide the kernel for all the complexity and all the color of Totton's stories. The core of the onion, as it were, is childhood innocence, either in its celebration or in its loss. When one sees through the kaleidoscope of word, color, emotive complexity, and gets a glimpse of that innocence, one has arrived at an understanding of the connection one instinctively feels while reading these stories. Totton's work strikes a familiar chord in anyone who has been a child, and that is everyone. The effect can be pleasant or unpleasant, depending on the reader's experiences and depending on the story. But in any case, one can expect, upon reading these tales, a revisiting of long-forgotten feelings and memories, like looking up into the clouds and seeing shapes you had left far, far behind one lazy summer day.

Welcome back.

A Fish Story

First appeared in *Realms of Fantasy Magazine*, October 2006.
Reprinted in *Fantasy: the Best of the Year: 2007*.

In the Vale of Brecon where the fishermen hunt their game amid deep and succulent cloud, where the yaks are pink, and where the maidens are all beautiful (with some exceptions) lived the grand old dowager, Lydia Batterfly.

Lydia Batterfly's greatest regret in life was her niece, Dagmar. Dagmar was neither inclined toward the practice of womanly etiquette, nor sufficiently attractive to be forgiven her disinclinations. Despite attendance at finishing school for two full years, she stubbornly refused to act like a lady. Worse, was her tendency to make a spectacle of herself over the most inappropriate things, most recently and deplorably, "that awful tower boy," as the dowager Batterfly referred to him.

"I don't know why you bother with him," said the dowager.

"His name is Henry," said Dagmar, "and I bother because he is *superb*."

"Not by *our* standards," said Lydia, by which she meant the standards of any sensible woman of good breeding and taste.

Henry, the bell tower boy was nearly seventeen with limbs as long as a spider monkey's and hair so short it barely colored his scalp. He went about town in simple white clothes, displaying no familial colors—the shameful apparel of a bastard. Henry's job was to climb the tower and play the fish until their echoes rang from the valley walls. There were five fish in the tower, caught from the Sonorous River, in the days when fish swam in rivers, by one Martidel Bayliss, the greatest fisherman in Brecon history. His enormous catches had been bronzed for posterity and hung in the tower where they were twice daily made to clatter amongst themselves in a semblance of music. Henry, the current bell tower boy, was recognized as one of the better practitioners of the art of fish-clattering. Dagmar had been in love with him from the moment she'd first seen him, trousers rolled up to his knees in the Friday Bog with a frog clutched in his fist, squeezing it just hard enough to make its eyes protrude.

The greatest disappointment in Dagmar's life was that Henry did not appear to be likewise infatuated with her. She ascribed this, given her deceptively unremarkable appearance, to his simply not having noticed her. She set about to remedy this.

On the eve of the coldest night of the year, just after the last murmur of the fish jangles had died away, Dagmar stationed herself below the tower looking up at the fish chamber fifty feet above. In her hands, she held her uncle's bangy-wurdle, salvaged from the dowager Batterfly's lumber room. Bangy-wurdles were the instruments of the insane, the bizarrely eccentric and the lower classes of society. No one of good breeding would even admit to owning one. The instrument produced a music often described as "a din of iniquity."

Practicing in secret, Dagmar had spent the summer learning to master the instrument. She reasoned it thusly: a piano was too difficult to drag to the town square, and a clarinet didn't allow for singing. And sing she did. She sang a song she had composed for her love, amidst daydreams of his froggy hands, his simian limbs and his days at play among the shining fish. At the close of the second verse, as she launched into the chorus, she saw a white face thrust out from the tower window.

"What's that fuss?" said Henry. "Are you ill?"

She finished the chorus and shouted up to him, "A song professing my love for you, dear Henry. Sit back and enjoy while I serenade you." And she continued to play what was later described by the town wag as, "the musical equivalent of a cat caught under a pram wheel."

Despite several pleas from around the square for Dagmar to hold her peace, she played on, singing of Henry's attributes.

"My what?" Henry shouted. "What are you saying?"

"Your glorious shining fingers," she shouted back.

There were some hoots of laughter from one of the nearby houses.

"Clear off," said Henry. "People will hear you."

"You are the most desirable man in the Vale of Brecon, and I am not going to stop until everyone knows it." Dagmar continued to play. She had not quite finished her fourth turn through the chorus when Henry, desperate to shut her up, emptied a water pail out of the tower window. The air was so cold that the cascade had nearly crystallized by the time it broke over Dagmar's head. Dagmar squeaked in shock and almost dropped the bangy-wurdle on the cobblestones.

"Now go home!" said Henry. And he banged the tower shutters closed.

Dagmar took a few moments to collect her wits, shaking the beads of ice from her coat and brushing them from the bangy-wurdle. Her hair was now frozen into points.

Lydia Batterfly's house abutted the square, and Dagmar retreated to it. There was no point in further stating her suit if Henry had closed the window. Unfortunately, as soon as she tried to open the front door, her wet hand froze fast to the metal knob. Try as she might, she could not get it free. Her shouts for assistance were met with answering shouts to shut up. Eventually, though, they drew her fondest friend Eora, the duchess' daughter, from the house next door. Eora was of that sensible type who are really quite wonderful in a pinch, though they tend to be dull and full of advice for living a good life at other times. On this occasion, Eora, who'd watched the entire spectacle from her bedroom window, came prepared carrying a bowl full of hot water from the kettle. The bowl had contained some exotic fruits which were now dumped over her mother's oak dining table. Eora proceeded to pour the steaming contents of the bowl over Dagmar's hand in an attempt to loosen it from the doorknob. The major difficulty being to stop herself laughing so hard that she dropped it.

"Yes, all right, all right," said Dagmar peeling her hand from the door handle. "It isn't funny. I mean, you have no idea what love does to a person. You'll see."

Though really, Dagmar thought, Eora was the sort of person who would fall in love—or something respectably close to it—with a suitable gentleman approved by her mother the duchess, and they would be wed in a ghastly ceremony in which Dagmar would be forced to attend in some abominable dress. Dagmar loathed dresses.

Word gets about in small places, and it wasn't long before Eora's mother, the Duchess, was informing Lydia Batterfly of what Dagmar had been up to while she had been out of town.

"She's sending me back to finishing school," said Dagmar to Eora that afternoon.

"Not again! That's what…The fourth time? What are you going to do?"

"Third, and I think she's going to find that Madame Loge will have nothing to do with me. She doesn't like to be reminded of her failings. They're so few and far between. As to what I'm going to do, I've thought of another plan."

"Plan?"

"To win Henry."

Eora stared at Dagmar and said nothing. Perhaps it was a tactful omission of words. When at last she spoke, she said, "What are you going to do?"

"Come with me and see," said Dagmar. She led the way down the center of the street, down the narrower alleyways of Brecon town, to Tyrone's Fishing Tackle Emporium.

"What on Earth?" Eora muttered.

Dagmar went inside and accosted the shop's proprietor. "I would like your best and strongest rod please."

"Yes, madam," said the proprietor. "We have a variety of—"

"The longest one you've got."

"Oh," said the merchant, and he led her to the window of the shop from which he pulled a small brass cylinder.

"That doesn't look very large, man," said Dagmar.

"If you would come outside." The merchant stepped out into the street and proceeded to extend the rod. The mechanism was a telescopic one. The merchant pulled each joint out, lengthening it until it stretched the entire length of the alley and protruded out over the High Street sidewalk. Curious onlookers peered at it warily and walked around it.

"Well?" said the merchant.

"I suppose if that's the longest one you've got, it will have to do," said Dagmar. "How much is it?"

"Oh, madam, workmanship like this… This is a one-of-a-kind, made on the Gwyntog Coast and designed after the one used by Martidel Bayliss who once fished with it in the ocean. It is the most beautiful piece of wo—"

"I'm amazed you're willing to part with it."

"I could be coerced," said the merchant. "But it would take a king's ransom."

"Far be it from me to part a man from his beloved rod. We'll look elsewhere, thanks."

"You will not find a larger or better rod in the entire Vale of Brecon."

"That's as may be, but I haven't got a king to ransom."

"Perhaps we could negotiate."

A price was settled, though the merchant claimed he would go bankrupt, and Dagmar claimed she would have no dowry, "Though without this, there would be no need for a dowry."

"Why, Dagmar?" said Eora. "What are you going to do?"

"I," said Dagmar, "am going to catch the Barbary Fish, and then—"

"You're out of your mind!" said the merchant. "You?! The best fisherman in the history of Brecon spent his entire career trying, and even he couldn't catch the Barbary Fish."

"Please," said Dagmar. "You interrupted me. As I was saying. I am going to catch the Barbary Fish and present him to Henry the tower boy as a token of my love."

"Dagmar…" said Eora.

"I know," said Dagmar. "I'll need bait."

Dagmar strode off waving her rod, now telescoped down to a more manageable twelve inches. Eora was forced to run to keep up with her. Dagmar led her to the fishing grounds at Leechfield. The day was gloriously clear, and there were several fishermen sprawled amid the long grasses, eyes following the spiderfloss of their fishing lines which disappeared into the sky, ending at their lures glinting from colorful balloons. High above them, the braver fishermen rode in baskets beneath larger balloons, harpoons held at the ready, sighting along the Vale for the cloud-wisps of fish-spoor.

Dagmar made straight for the oldest and raggedest of the veteran fishermen at Leechfield and without preamble, said, "If you were to try for the Barbary Fish, where would you set your line and how would you bait your hook?"

The man looked at Dagmar and snorted. "Five miles of golden spiderfloss, four of silver. And for a lure, the blue stained glass from the window of Epiphany. And everyone knows the Barbary Fish frequents the hills at Devil's End."

"You've never tried to catch him yourself?"

"I'm not mad."

"Well then, thank you, sir," said Dagmar.

That night, someone broke the Epiphany window. It was later determined that a stone had been thrown through it. Three days after this Dagmar's aunt found the family tapestry bundled up in the cupboard under the stairs. Half of it had been unraveled, and the gold and silver threads had all been pulled out. None of the servants would own up to doing it.

Shortly afterwards, Dagmar became suddenly attentive at her macramé and crochet lessons. Madam Loge began to entertain cautious hopes for her reform.

Ten days later, Dagmar appeared dripping wet at Eora's door.

"You'll have to help me," said Dagmar. She led her friend to Leechfield where a gathering of fishermen were ringed around the convex, glittering side of an enormous fish.

"Is that the Barbary—"

"Well, no actually," said Dagmar. "But it's quite a respectable one I think. It dragged me across Leechfield and all along the Sonorous River. Do you see this?" Dagmar proudly displayed a missing tooth. "Came out when I hit the Bridge. No one warned me it might take me up. Anyway, it dropped me in the sea and I suppose it expected me to let go, but I wasn't going to give it the satisfaction. I worried it about a bit, then it seemed to tire, enough that I could wind it in close enough to start biffing and kicking it. It got the message and went to ground here. Which was lucky, as I didn't fancy landing in the quarry."

"What are you going to do with it?" said Eora.

"Have it bronzed, of course. It's easily bigger than any of the ones in the tower now."

Eora's eyes grew wide, but she didn't comment. The look of fanatical determination in Dagmar's eyes stilled her tongue.

Henry, as it happened, was neither pleased, nor impressed when Dagmar, accompanied by a parade of dancing acrobats and men in military costume, presented the bronzed fish to him at the door of the tower.

"That won't fit up the steps," he said.

"We'll hoist it from outside," said Dagmar. "This is a gift to you, a token of my esteem."

"Look," said Henry. He glanced at the acrobats somersaulting crosswise in front of him and lowered his voice. "Stop doing this."

"Doing what?"

"Giving me things, publicly declaring your feelings for me."

"Martidel Bayliss didn't stop trying to catch the Barbary Fish and look at him."

"Right, but he never caught it, though, did he?" said Henry.

"No, but he spent his *entire life* trying. Isn't that utterly marvelous? That is dedication, Henry, as I am dedicated in my love for you."

"But I don't love you. I don't even like you. What you're doing… It's embarrassing me. It's insulting. Stop it."

Dagmar's face fell, and her brow furrowed in thought. "Very well." She bowed. "But take the fish."

"So, you have seen sense at last," said Eora as they sipped wine in the conservatory.

Dagmar shrugged. "If you mean have I given up, then no. Not at all."

"But he ordered you to leave him alone."

"Ah, yes. And that is because I have not done enough to earn his love. I have not sacrificed enough, I have not suffered enough."

"And you think he has not suffered enough either." Eora sighed. "This is fatuous. It's senseless."

"No. Senseless is in the country of Giving Up. What is the purpose of living if I can't pursue him? If I stopped, it would mean I didn't really love him. And I do."

"He says he doesn't love you."

"If he really believes that…"

"Yes?" Eora leaned closer.

"…then I haven't been trying hard enough."

Exasperated, Eora proclaimed, "A woman pursuing a man is a scandal. I think you are doing it to mortify your aunt Lydia."

"I am doing it for the glory," said Dagmar. "A glory most women are afraid to taste."

For a few weeks nothing new transpired, except that Dagmar began to pay rapt attention to her art instructor. Then one morning, a large mural was found covering the front of Dagmar's house. It depicted a man, endowed with yak-like proportions, strutting atop an enormous tower from which a golden fish hung.

The next day, Henry of the bell tower asked the swineherd's daughter to marry him.

"Now, even you must admit defeat," said Eora.

"Not at all," said Dagmar. "This girl, what do you know about her?"

"She's very beautiful."

"Ah," said Dagmar, "But did she earn her beauty, or did she happen upon it by way of the womb? What has she done to be *worthy* of Henry?"

"Well nothing," said Eora, "except I suppose that he likes her. And perhaps she was patient enough to let him make up his own mind about that, and doesn't wake him at midnight singing his praises, or drop uninvited fish and acrobats in his lap."

"No," said Dagmar. "It can't be that simple. If he truly believes he loves her, then it's because I haven't tried hard enough."

Eora happened to meet Henry in Evelyn Street the next afternoon. They greeted each other cordially, if cautiously, like two people who share an embarrassing complaint.

"It won't work," said Eora. "I mean, if that's why you've done it."

"What?"

"Proposing to another girl. In fact, I think you've spurred her on to try even harder to win you."

"Tell her from me that she can go to hell," Henry muttered. "Tell her I'll send her there myself if she doesn't stop it." He stalked off.

Eora went off to do as he asked, but at the door to Dagmar's house, she stopped. Her hand, lifted to tap on the door, dropped to her side, and she regarded it pensively. What was the use talking to Dagmar? She wouldn't listen to reason.

A few days later, Dagmar was sitting on the bank of the Sonorous River, working out a plot to stop Henry's wedding. She was planning the speech she would make when the minister asked if there were any objections to the wedding. Of course there were. Anyone could see that Henry had become engaged solely to annoy her and not because he loved this other girl.

Dagmar was deep in thought writing her speech when a shadow fell across the parchment. She looked up, but instead of an obtrusive cloud, she saw a man looming over her.

"You're in my light," said Dagmar. "Move off."

"*You* are my light," said the man.

Dagmar, whose head had bowed to the task of writing almost before the words were out of her mouth looked up suddenly. "What?"

"Lady for whose sake alone I breathe, listen while I tell you that I adore you."

It was the fisherman from Leechfield. The old, ragged man who'd told her about baiting hooks.

"You're cracked!" said Dagmar. "You're twice my age for a start. And anyway, in case you hadn't noticed, and you must be deaf, mad and stupid if you haven't, I'm in love with Henry the tower boy."

"Henry is engaged to the swineherd's daughter."

"That's what he thinks," said Dagmar, standing up and brushing the heads of grasses from her cloak.

"He is betrothed," said the fisherman. "Whereas I am not. We are better suited to each other." He began to follow Dagmar as she made her way back to the square.

"Don't you have fish to catch?" said Dagmar.

"None more beautiful than you, and none more sly and worthy than you." As they walked, the fisherman's voice rose so that people in the square turned to watch them.

"Look," said Dagmar, rounding on him, "Look here, back off. I've told you to go. Everyone knows where my heart belongs."

The fisherman fell to his knees. "Most glorious girl, listen to me while I declare my love for you in front of these people, for no one could be more worthy of a fisherman's love than the woman who tried for the Barbary Fish."

"Yes, yes, all right. Everyone knows I didn't get him, but thanks for bringing it to their attention. Now clear off."

The fisherman grabbed hold of the hem of Dagmar's cloak so that she had to jerk it free. She turned and stalked off.

The fisherman followed her, tossing glass-glazed fish scales over her head. "A tribute," he said.

Someone nearby sniggered. Dagmar had to make an undignified run to her house, slamming and bolting the door behind her.

"It isn't funny, Eora," said Dagmar. She had to raise her voice to be heard over the wailing coming from below the window as the Leechfield fisherman serenaded her.

"I think it's romantic," said Eora. "Why don't you consider him?"

"Look, Eora, there are two kinds of people in the world. The Pursuers and the Pursued. And the Pursuers neither like nor wish to be pursued. It is an insult to their nature."

"I heard that Henry proposed to the swineherd's daughter," said Eora. "She didn't pursue him at all."

Dagmar frowned. "Do you know, that man is singing off-key. I didn't sing off-key when I serenaded Henry…did I?"

Eora shrugged. "I couldn't really tell over Henry's shouting at you to shut up."

"And at least I composed an original song," said Dagmar. "This raving nit is borrowing an old chestnut and trotting it out like it's the latest thing. He's doing a poor job of it all around." Dagmar shot to her feet and marched to the bathroom, filled a tub with the coldest water she could manage and wrestled it back to the window. She tipped the water out of the window onto the singing fisherman.

"Hmmm," she said. "Perhaps I ought to learn from my own mishaps."

Eora brightened. "Yes!"

Then Dagmar picked up the potted plant next to the window and tipped out over the ledge as well. "Yes, the water makes the soil stick quite well," she said, peering down. "It *does* pay to learn from one's mistakes."

The next day in church, the Leechfield fisherman presented Dagmar with a garland of the finest cerise yak's hair. Yak's hair garlands were considered *de rigueur* at the time. Dagmar stood up in the pew and shouted, "Stop! I cannot think of anything more annoying, more aggravating, more infuriating than your pursuit of me when I have clearly told you that I am not interested. You are an ass. An ass' ass, and your attention to me is insulting." As she said this, her eyes happened upon Henry who was standing by the door to the tower, about to ring his fish to signify the end of the service.

Dagmar's cheeks turned a shade reminiscent of the most fashionable yak's hair, and she walked out.

Henry married the swineherd's daughter without incident and they lived in comfortable married squabblehood, his wife being unencumbered with the notion that she had married a perfect man.

Dagmar failed finishing school in spectacular fashion for the third time and finished up a merry spinster, living on the outskirts of town. On fine days, she can sometimes be seen using her famous brass rod. She has yet to catch the Barbary Fish.

The Leechfield fisherman moved to the City where he bought a suite of rooms in one of the city towers from which the trawling was more rewarding than from his former, cheaper lodgings in a down-to-earth bungalow. It was an expensive purchase, but affordable to one whom has benefited from the dowry of a duchess' daughter.

The fish served at Eora's wedding fed six hundred people.

The Man with the Seahorse Head

Published in *Commonwealth Short Stories* CD 2007–2008.
Regional Winner (for Canada & the Caribbean)
of the Commonwealth Short Story Competition.

The man with the seahorse head strides jauntily down the Promenade, umbrella in hand, twirling rays of ice cream colors: cream, chocolate, and strawberry. The mist blows sideways so the umbrella is this side of useless, but he holds it up anyway, because that's what one does with umbrellas.

At the midway the megaphone moans, the arcades wail, and the air is thick with the enticing smell of hot fat and the sea. The man with the seahorse head passes the fairground and climbs down the steps to the beach, which is, owing to the weather, almost deserted. He walks along the beach, following the headland to its tip where the sea, now rising, laps at it. He collapses his umbrella and spikes it into the sand.

He opens his white coat and unbuttons his waistcoat. Beneath it, his brood pouch pulses. He opens the pouch. He lifts out his youngest child. It squalls while he holds it, dangling by a gossamer leg, and though its eyes are not fully formed (its eyelids are still sealed) it weeps tiny silver beads.

This is his fourth child: his only son. The man with the seahorse head has high hopes for this one. Its mother was a mermaid he found in an abandoned water butt.

He has not named his son yet. He has learned the hard way that naming a child early might well be a waste of a name, and he is running short of good ones.

His first child, Marilyn, died in his brood pouch a month after hatching. His second, Penny, was attacked in the playground when he took her to the park. Two children, intrigued and capriciously provoked by her blue crystal skin and shining eyes, bounced her off a wall and smashed her to pieces. Her bones broke into perfect spheres, and the children stole them to use as marbles.

His third child, Anna, had a seashell on her back. She learned to sing *Frère Jacques* and to dance in sunbeams. She grew big enough to be let out of his brood pouch when he went out. But one morning he came home to find her shriveled up in the sink, the stem of a daisy gripped in her brittle fingers.

The man with the seahorse head now holds his fourth child. He spies an emerald filament twisting around his son's leg. He isn't sure whether he ought to pull it out, or whether it's part of him, and he should leave it be. He's growing and changing so quickly, one never knows. It might be an effect of the sea air. He wants to believe this—that the sea will be good to him.

The man with the seahorse head drops his son into the sea. He has been keeping his children too long, killing them with love when he should have let them go. Maybe this one will live and maybe he won't, but the man with the seahorse head can hope.

As he watches his son flick like a minnow through the waves, in clouds of suspended sand, he decides to call him 'Sparkle.' He has been saving that name for a good, long time.

It is raining in earnest now. The man with the seahorse head looks out to sea one more time then he turns and walks along the beach. It is good weather for courting mermaids.

Flatrock Sunners

Appeared in *Black Static #12*.

My father was a great man, once upon a time. I am often told this. But for as long as I've known him, and for as long as I can remember, he was no such thing. I have memories—distant ones—of him being happy, of him knowing who I was, maybe even loving me, but ever since he went away the first time, he has never been happy, or anything at all. I blame the Flatrock Sunners.

I've always known there was something in the things I heard but didn't quite understand, growing up. The way my mother never used certain words, or went quiet when someone said the wrong ones. The way she packed me off to live with Aunt Henny at my grandparents' house, in my last year of high school, not long after my father went away again.

Sitting in bed, I lean back against the cracked plaster of the guest bedroom wall. This was my father's bedroom when he was a kid. There's a photo of him on the wall, smiling and holding up a football trophy, the same trophy that's sitting dusty on the dresser. He was a star kicker in high school, my dad.

I sit here in his room, and I write my secrets in the book my mother gave me before she sent me away. I feel a troubling ache in my neck as I write. The sun shines in the window this time of day, but I feel the cold in little puffs through the crack in the wall behind me.

Somewhere it's warm. Somewhere it's good and quiet. Somewhere people are enjoying themselves. Somewhere that isn't here.

In the front hallway, the phone rings, and I stop writing, pen hovering over the paper. Aunt Henny answers it, and I can tell from the way she lowers her voice that I don't want to know what she's saying. She speaks now the way she turns her head when I'm in the room, with a gentle, tactful avoidance, like she wishes her messed-up nephew Danny wasn't here.

It runs in families, apparently.

Sometimes, if I think about it too hard, I start to hear my dad's voice in the screeching of a train's wheels, or in the slamming of a door, or in Dad's trophy buzzing on the dresser as a truck drives by. When that happens, it sounds like he's screaming at me, like he did the last time I went to visit him in hospital. Like he didn't know who I was, like he hated me.

Now I can hear his voice again, and I have to get out, to fill my head with deliberate sounds, ones that *I* make, to drown out the ones I imagine. As soon as Aunt Henny puts the receiver down with a *ching*, all the words she may have said are there in the room with me, and my heart won't let me be. It drums me off the bed, and I'm pacing the room up and down trying to catch up. I have to get out, out of the room, out of the house, and I'm running down the back lawn, thumping my feet on the grass to stop the words, pounding the board fence as I go to drown them out, down the long slope of the grass to where it disappears under the river.

I sit on the sagging lawn chair holding my head, kicking the metal leg of the chair to hear it ping and filling the air with my breathing. The river's flowing quiet here, barely rippling, but upstream a bit, it's showing its teeth around three chunky limestone slabs. I've seen those slabs a hundred times. I used to spot turtles riding their backs and fix their stillness in my mind while I watched the water split around them.

Today it's cold but the sun's shining on them, and they're more *present* to me than they've ever been before. When I look away, a black shadow seethes in front of my eyes. When I look back, I see something lying on top of one of those slabs. Too big, wrong shape for a turtle. I think maybe it's a wet log. Until it moves. The movement's a casual back and forth. Not wind, not water—muscle-driven movement. It settles a little further down the slab, like it's stretching out in obvious pleasure.

I find myself standing at the water's edge. Whatever it is moves again. A dark streak, a whip-crack of sound, and the thing that was on the boulder is now knee-deep in the river, bent in half at the waist pinning something under the water with his hands. I feel a flash of panic suddenly, because he looks so *wrong*, like something you'd pay to see floating in a jar. He's human-sized, but too long in the body, shoulders hunched and bent like they're coiled up under the skin on his back. His thin tail flicks back and forth as he struggles with the thing in the water. The thing he's holding down is ripping the water white.

A scream like a kettle on the boil sounds across the river. On the opposite shore stands a kid in orange, about my age, holding a whistle in his mouth and blowing it hard. He spits the whistle out, and shouts, "Fair play, Basker!"

The dark creature in the river does not look up as he speaks. "Keep out of this, Imago."

The kid crosses the river, arms swinging in an easy strut like he's walking a red carpet. Basker looks up in time to catch the kid's foot under his chin. Doesn't look like much of a kick, but Basker flips up and back, corkscrewing in mid-air, the whole impossible length of him. He lands, scrambling for footing, halfway up the slab. Basker straightens up, and his tail swings down and twitches capriciously. Water shoots up in the kid's direction. I swear, it's like he's giving the kid the finger. Then, *flick-flick* like a minnow, Basker's on the bank, and *flick*, he's into the trees, a glimpse of shadow, then he's gone.

The thing Basker was pinning down sits bolt upright with a cough of water. He's deep purple and shimmering, like a grackle. He stands, slicks his damp bristles back along his head and looks around him. He sees the kid in orange.

"Slick," says the kid with a nod. "Pay up."

Slick drives his hand into his pocket. He's wearing something like a pair of waders, at least the pockets seem to go down to his knees, and his arm disappears past his elbow. He pulls out an orange glass bottle shaped like an hourglass, and he lobs it to the kid. Then he slips back into the water, slow and quiet, leaving an expanding arrowhead of ripples along the surface.

I move up the riverbank to get a closer look at the kid. He's a black kid about my age, wearing an orange jacket, golden sunglasses, and a ballcap on sideways. He's standing under the weeping willow on the opposite bank. As I watch him, he holds the hourglass bottle, his finger and thumb circling its waist. He twists the cap to open it and drains the bottle in two enormous, theatrical swigs. Then he snaps his fingers, and the bottlecap buzzes over the water, skipping twice like a stone and sinks, about a foot from where I'm standing. Then the kid turns and springs up, catching a low-hanging branch, and he swings from this into the upper canopy. That and a glint of orange glass in his other hand is the last I see of him.

The water numbs my hand when I plunge it in to pick up the bottlecap. It shines green under the water, but when I pull it out, it's bright orange like a traffic light. Printed on the inside of the cap are words I can only make out when I'm back in the house peering through Aunt Henny's magnifying lens: 'Flatrock Sunners.'

I feel a little betrayed then. Because the Sunners were something my dad told me about back when he was still okay, and I thought they belonged just to us.

When I was really young, before things went bad, I used to visit my grandparents, and Dad and I would sit out behind their house. Once, he showed me how to catch crayfish in the river. He wouldn't let me wade out to the big white rocks. The current was too strong out there. That's what my grandmother said. But Dad said it was because they belonged to the Flatrock Sunners. Basker, Slick, Slander, Imago. There were more, but I don't remember their names.

I used to squint at those slabs, but I never saw anything on them but turtles and branches.

"Oh, they're there," Dad would insist.

"Can other people see them?"

"Sure, Danny. Sometimes… When they dream, when they're in love, when they're very sick, after something bad happens."

He would tell me stories about them while I sat on the riverbank. I don't remember them now. It's hard enough remembering that he used to be okay.

A week later, I'm sitting against the chain-link fence behind the school. I'm squeezing the bottlecap in my fist. I like the way it makes my tendons ache. I've been doing it all week, and I have scabs on both palms now. I like looking at them. It takes my mind off the other guys playing basketball nearby. And helps me ignore the girls watching them.

I hear a rustle of leaves, and down he drops out of the tree overhead, the kid from the river, landing on the asphalt next to me. He straightens up, adjusts his ballcap.

"Hey, friend," he says.

"Hey," I say. My voice sounds a little busted; I don't use it much.

"What's with you?" he says, nudging me.

I shrug. "Ask them," I nod to the guys playing basketball. "They'll tell you what's wrong with me."

"Nothing's wrong with you. Something's right with you, that's why I'm talking to you. People they call nuts are the ones that can see. Not those guys. What do you call them that can't see what's right in front of them?"

"Idiots?" I say and laugh.

"There you go."

"I'm Danny," I say.

"Imago." He shakes my hand.

"That really your name?"

"Why not?" He grins.

He has a good, honest face, and there's no judgement or unkindness in his expression. His eyes are steady on me though, and it feels awkward to be looked at like that, so I look back to where the other guys are playing ball. The girls are talking to each other, but they're really checking out the guys.

"Those girls don't think those guys are idiots," I say, "but they wouldn't give me the time of day."

"You don't need the time of day from *them*," says Imago. "You got me now."

"No offense, but when I said they wouldn't give me the time of day, I didn't mean…*the time of day*." I feel a smile cracking my face.

Imago's expression grows serious and intent. Across the street through the link fence I see what he's looking at: a heavy-set guy leaning against a lamppost with a paper under his arm. He's completely bald, and there's something wrong with his head that I can't put my finger on from this distance.

"Slander," Imago mutters.

"What?"

"Bad news, that guy."

"You know him?"

Imago simply looks. There's a stillness about the man across the street. He doesn't fidget with the paper; he doesn't move at all, but he's looking across the road in our direction. At us. The unsafe feeling comes back to me all of a sudden like the echo of my dad's voice.

A polished, white car rolls up to the curb, slow. The driver's door drifts open, and someone steps out. I get the impression of a lot of leg, white-blonde hair, and a slim dark body. Moving like she knows what she's doing, walking towards Slander. She's nothing like the girls by the basketball court; she's in another league. I still feel the panic, but now it's mixed with mesmerizing energy.

"Wow," I say. "She could give me the time of day any time of day." And I haven't even seen her face yet. "What's a girl like that want with a creep like him?"

"Not what you think, man," says Imago, and I feel his hand on me. He pulls me clear of the fence and drags me around the corner of the school.

"Hey!"

"Forget them," he says.

I feel angry with him. "I just want a look." I start back toward the fence, and he steps in front of me and puts his hand on my chest. Then I see the worry in his expression and the sadness too. That stops me. "Okay," I say, and hold up my hands in surrender.

The bell rings for afternoon classes.

"Catch ya," says Imago, then he's gone, and I'm standing there alone and frustrated.

For the first few days after that I'm looking over my shoulder every other second, seeing a blink of orange in the corner of my eye. Once, staring out the window in class because I hear a rustling in the tree outside, I see golden leaves flying off the branches, shaken loose, and then I think I see a hand lift towards me, like a signal. I don't know. Maybe I want to see it. No one else seems to notice.

I resent Imago for showing me a ray of light and then shutting the door. To hell with him, I think.

That night, I'm trying to sleep. Beside me, the brass clock ticks. It's the kind with the number tabs that flip down when the time changes. I'm watching it because it's 9:59, and all the numbers are about to change, when suddenly the numbers aren't numbers any more but eyes looking back at me through holes in the 9's. I turn the clock around. The tabs flip down, and it sounds like mechanical eyelids blinking. I get up, wrap the clock in a sweater I will never wear again and bury it in the back of a drawer. I can still hear it ticking.

The next day, I'm walking home from school, and I pass the board fence surrounding the patio at Annabelle's. A swanky restaurant. My dad took me there once, when he was still okay.

I trail my fingers along the red line of spray paint across the boards, but when I feel something smooth and cold in the wood, I stop. There's a knot in the wood, nice and round, right the way through the board. The hole's filled with glass, curved like a lens. I look through.

On the other side is the patio at Annabelle's, the way I remember it except, because it's October, the chairs are stacked by the door, and the tables are put away. Except for one table and two chairs in the center of the patio.

There's the girl I saw the other day. Close up, she looks a few years older than me, perched on the edge of the chair, sitting with her knees tucked under her chin. The way a girl can sit only if she's thin and small. But she's more than a girl; she's a woman. Her bare legs are smooth and rounded, with curves exactly where a girl's supposed to have them. From where I'm standing, she looks small enough for me to pick her up and put her in my pocket where I can keep her warm. Her hair's sugar-white and sparkling. She's wearing a short, black dress, shining down the sides with buttons like candied cherries. Her shoulders are bare and the straps of her dress are like a cat's cradle.

Sitting across from her is an enormous guy, and when I see him, I recognize him from outside the school. Slander. I see what it was about his head that bothered me that day; he has no ears. There are holes leading into his skull, but there's no trace of anything external, not even stumps sticking out to show where his ears should be.

His scalp is smooth and shiny and white. He's chewing something with loud, sticky sounds. His mouth is so wide and his jaw so thin that his chin looks like a platter for his head.

The girl speaks. "How much longer, Slander? How much *longer*?"

Slander speaks, deep-voiced, his mouth clotted with food. "Ah, the bait's lament. Patience, Idette. We'll have him by and by." He looks up from his plate and I swear, he sees me, stares right at me. I feel panic start to come up, like vomit.

Run, you idiot! I think, but I can't move.

"Have yourself an eyeful, young man," says Slander. "Enjoy the view." Then he laughs around the stickiness in his mouth.

The sound breaks me free. I stagger back from the fence, holding my chest, feeling darting pains. I make myself run across the parking lot to the convenience store on the corner. I stand inside staring at the magazine rack, telling myself I'm safe. But I don't feel safe at all.

A few days later I'm walking home across the park, and something solid and supple drops onto the footpath beside me. I keep walking, pretending to be cool.

"Hey, friend," says Imago. He doesn't miss a step. He's brought a pile of leaves down with him, and they drift off his jacket as we walk along.

"Hey, stranger," I say. "I missed you."

Imago shoves me, kind of playfully, kind of not, and starts off down the path again. I catch up to him.

"Where were you?" I ask.

"I never went anywhere."

We fall into step. Then Imago pulls up short and whistles like a bomb dropping.

Slander's standing on the path in front of us. He looks different today, dressed in a sharp suit. Less sinister, more…like a businessman. He walks up to us like he's got every right to. The way he looks, I'm almost expecting him to tell me off.

"Hello, Danny," he says to me.

"Back off, Slander," says Imago.

The sunlight's quivering on Slander's skin. "Think he's your boy, do you, Imago?" says Slander. "Methinks he's his own boy. Aren't you, Danny?" He holds out his hand like he wants to shake mine.

I take a step back.

"Why are you wasting your time with him, Danny?" says Slander.

"He's my friend," I say.

"I can offer you more than friendship," says Slander. "More than he can give you."

"You just want to cut him down, Slander," says Imago.

"Never mind my predilections," says Slander.

"I *do*," says Imago. I hear the crisp snap as he smacks Slander's proffered hand away.

Slander sighs like it's a lost cause and walks past us.

When he's gone, I look at Imago. "What did he mean?"

Imago shoves his hands in his pockets and shakes his head. "You don't want to get into that," he says. "Slander's sick."

"That girl that was with him before…?"

"Forget her."

"Did she used to be *your* girl?"

"Lay off, Danny," says Imago. He unfolds his sunglasses and puts them on, but not before I see the hurt in his eyes.

"Is she Slander's girl now?"

"Uh-huh. But not the way you think. She's his the way you don't want to know."

I figure he'll give me a hard time if I argue, so I let it go. He walks with me as far as the tennis courts, but there's an awkward feeling between us. I guess he picks up on it. He stops under a tree and pulls himself up to the nearest branch. On his way, he squeezes my shoulder, like he's giving me some bad news or something. Then he disappears into the patchwork of leaves. I listen to the rustling until it could have been just the wind.

It's a cold November afternoon, and I'm out just to get out. The leaves are nearly gone, and I haven't seen Imago in a while. I'm crossing over the bridge to downtown. It's so cold there's a skin of ice spreading from the river banks. In the band of open water, the current's running sharp. Water sounds different when it's cold.

I see them before I'm halfway across the bridge. She's leaning back, looking like a Parisienne model with her arms stretched out along the rail behind her. Slander's standing next to her.

I want to turn and leave. And I want just as much to walk up to them. So I just stop and stand there on the bridge a few paces away until Slander acknowledges me.

"I knew you'd come," he says. "You're curious. You want to know about it."

"About what?" I say.

"You know what I'm talking about," says Slander. "A young man your age. You like looking through my lens, hmm? It's easy to arrange if you want to do more than just look."

I know what he's offering, know that I'm not likely to get it any other way, not without having to wait or ask or beg for it, maybe not even then.

I glance at the girl surreptitiously, to see how she feels about this, but she's leaning back and staring at the sky, doesn't look as if she cares.

"How much?" I say.

"Hmm," he says. "Why don't I think about that? Perhaps we can come to an arrangement."

I don't like the sound of this. "I don't know."

Slander shrugs. "Think about it. We'll be here."

I walk across the bridge, leaving them there in the quiet cold.

He gives me time to fantasize, to stew, to ferment. I can say 'no' once, but in my head, he offers again and again, and I can't keep telling him no.

By the end of the week, I want that girl so badly that I don't care what it costs me. A week after our meeting, I'm heading back to the bridge. Hoping Slander's not there, praying he is.

As I'm cutting across the park, I hear someone walking in step behind me. I turn.

"Hey," says Imago.

I'm feeling distracted. I don't want to talk to him now. "So…you just show up whenever you feel like?" I say. "Where were you last week?"

I can see the bridge now. Slander and the girl are there waiting for me. She looks more inviting and unattainable than I remembered.

"Danny," says Imago. "I can't protect you if you go to him."

"Quit holding me back," I say.

"Don't go, Danny," he says.

I can hear the hurt in his voice. It makes me angry and frustrated. I head for the bridge. Imago doesn't follow me.

I go up to Slander where he's standing, looking approving. "Okay," I say.

Slander pockets his hands, jingles something in there eagerly. "Let's say we wager for her?" he says. "Winner take all. If you win, you get her for nothing."

I told myself that I would refuse if his price was too high. But I knew I would have agreed to whatever he offered.

"Not now," says Slander. "After you've finished, of course."

I absorb the implications, staring at the girl.

"I can tell you're eager," says Slander. "No need to delay. Come on."

He leads me down the pathway that runs to the back of the park. The snow's melted into crusty muck that blackens my shoes. Slander and the girl are wearing black boots and don't seem to mind.

I assumed Slander would provide a room, but he leads me instead to the petting zoo that abuts onto the park.

It's Sunday, and the zoo is closed. Slander unlocks the gate, and we go in. Down an even muddier track we come to a breezeway running between two sheds. Slander stops a discreet distance away and jingles his pockets again.

"Go on, Idette," he says. "The boy's waiting."

Her expression doesn't change as she steps through the mud into the breezeway. She waits for me, leaning back against the corrugated metal wall of the shed. I go to her. Close up, I notice that her white hair is yellow at the roots and frayed at the ends, chopped rough. She's wearing black silk, but her waistcoat's trimmed down the sides with fake round rubies.

I'm not a tall guy, but I'm head and shoulders taller than she is, and what there is of her is nearly all leg. Above the waist, there's nothing to her. I could have circled her waist with my hands and then some, and I try, and her jeweled flanks click under my palms.

Can I say 'no' to this? Not if I try, and I'm disinclined to try. Very disinclined. It's hard enough putting off what I want to do until Slander moves out of sight. I feel like I've waited forever; I can't wait any longer.

The wind blows through the breezeway with the smell of mouldy hay, sound of a garbage bag rattling, letting my hands stray down her body and the silk shreds into strips under my hands, red ribbons striping the wall, blowing in the wind like kite-tails. Under her waistcoat, the straps of her dress gummy as spidersilk, the bones of her spine like wooden blocks on a string hitting the wall behind, and I'm out of breath and the buttons are chinging on the metal, the smell of garbage and pollen popping from flowers, and the air's hot and sparkling, and I feel like a cored apple and, I yell because I can't stop, and she's swelling against me, and her breasts split like boiled peaches, and she bursts like a ripe pumpkin dropped from the sky.

And I'm standing there, bent over, stuff running out of my mouth and nose I don't know what, like I've taken a bite out of my cheek and got bone in it too, and it's all down the front of me, slicking the wall like oil and gravel, and I can barely walk, but I get out of there.

At the mouth of the breezeway Slander is smoking a cigar. As I come out, he applauds, slowly. "Congratulations," he says.

And I stagger past him because he doesn't matter, he can't mess me up more than I already am.

Somewhere along the way, I realize I've busted a tooth. The sharp edge of it slices my tongue. I get home, start pulling my clothes off before the door shuts behind me, smearing them up the hallway on my way to the bathroom, shower on full-blast and flailing to get it off. *Off!* Standing there with my head bowed, bloody spit drooling off my lip, feeling my pulse in my gums. My hair pretzel-hard and twisted catching my fingers like brambles. I feel for gashes, seams, open flesh, but apart from my mouth, there's nothing. How can I be unbroken, uncut?

I crawl out of the shower, still spraying behind me. My pants, my shirt, are slopped on the white tile, them and those orange, stringy gobs of I-don't-know-what. What did I do to her? I pick them up one at a time, and they hang from my fingernails, and I drop them into the tub. I'm tasting burnt bone, a sloughing at the back of my throat. I spit into the sink, but it won't come. I cough and retch, and a slimy red button, like a candied cherry clicks into the sink. I look in the mirror and speak to a stranger.

"You're a man now, you complete fuck," I tell myself. And then I weep.

I can't fall asleep. At midnight, the phone rings like sudden thunder. I shoot bolt upright. The lights flick on in the hall outside my room, and I hear Aunt Henny's voice. She sounds worried, and I don't want to hear what she's saying. I feel so alone. The bedroom's empty, but I search it anyway, even part the curtains and peer into the darkness outside. But the trees are bare and hide no secrets.

The next day, I find out what the phone call was about. When I come home from school, my dad is sitting in the living room. He's wrapped in a comforter. He looks so old and strange, just sitting, staring out through the glass in the patio doors. His hair is all gray now. There's a softness about him, like he's on the verge of collapsing inwards. He's wearing a gray sweater, not the gown they made him wear in the hospital. It makes him look worse, somehow. When someone's in a hospital gown, you *expect* them to look sick. In normal clothes, you expect them to look okay.

I don't know why he's here. Maybe Aunt Henny believes that with some rest and a peaceful setting, he'll regain some hint of his former greatness.

I remember him showing me how to tie my shoelaces, telling me stories. I have a feeling that what he is now is the best he's ever going to be. Looking at him, I feel scared.

If he recognizes me, he gives no sign. I don't know what he's going to say or if he's even going to talk, but I have to say it.

"Dad? I saw the Flatrock Sunners." I dig the bottlecap out of my pocket. Orange so bright it's almost glowing. "For real, Dad. See?" I show him.

He stares, not blinking, not moving. At least he isn't screaming at me, like before.

"Basker, Slick, Imago, Dad. I saw them."

I'm lucky, maybe. He seems to hear me. And he looks at me, really sad. "I'm so sorry, Danny." He sounds like he's trying to comfort me. For just a second, then he's gone again, doing the thousand-mile stare through my chest like I'm made of glass. I look behind me, but there's nothing there.

Aunt Henny comes in. She doesn't look at me. I guess after singing my dad's praises for so long, she's embarrassed to be confronted with… this.

I start to laugh, like a hiccup, and I can't stop.

That night, something wakes me. I sit up in bed, feeling plaster dust settling over my face. I sneeze. Somewhere upstairs, I hear someone yelling. I get out of bed, step out into the hallway where it's warmer. It's my dad's voice, shouting, "Flatrock Sunners! Flatrock Sunners!"

I slam my door, but it doesn't drown out his voice. I sit on the edge of my bed, and I press my hands to the sides of my head, trying to force it out.

I feel something nudge my shoulder. Imago is there, sitting cross-legged on the end of my bed.

"Talk to me," I say.

So he does. I don't listen to his words, just the rhythm of them, or the off-rhythm. It's enough to work my dad's words deeper down so I don't feel them as strong.

After a time, my heart slows down.

"Thanks," I mumble. "For knowing what to say."

"I've been there," he says quietly.

"Been where?"

"Where you're going. I know," he says, really quiet.

"You're too good to be true," I say. "How do I know you're even real?"

"'cause somebody's gotta love you, Danny boy," he says, and he punches me playfully.

I avoid the park and the bridge all through the next week. I take the long way home, walking under the trees when I can. It feels safer there.

But eventually, one day, I hear heavy footsteps behind me. I keep walking, pretending I don't know he's there. I catch a glimpse of something orange off by the edge of the trees. I'm not sure, because I look away fast. I don't want to draw Slander's eye towards it.

Slander keeps his distance until I reach the bandstand, and then I feel him clasp me tight between my shoulder and neck. I didn't know he was that close. I go rigid.

"This matter of payment," says Slander in my ear, and he forces me up the steps of the bandstand.

Once there, he clears a space in the snow down to the blue boards with the back of his foot. He makes me kneel in the snow beside the patch he's cleared, and then he squats down opposite me; I feel snow melting under my shins.

Slander's smirking at me. "It's time we had our little game. Winner take all."

I hear a step on the boards of the bandstand. Crunch, more like, and over Slander's shoulder I see a couple of long, white legs, all shining. Above the legs is something narrower than ribcage, wider than spine and all white and black and white criss-crossing over it. When I see the head, I know it's Idette, or used to be. Just her pretty, bored eyes, not looking at anything. I can see her breathing, a rippling in the harlequin mess of her body.

"She cleans up pretty, doesn't she?" says Slander.

She stands between us. She has no feet. Her legs run to points in the snow. She blinks and I can't look at her.

"I'll begin, shall I?" says Slander. With his unnaturally white hand, Slander reaches out and grasps Idette at the joint of her knee. Her skin tears and he pulls something long and white and very slender out of her. He keeps pulling on it until it comes right the way out and then he drops it, glistening, onto the snow between us. It's the bone from Idette's leg. Idette is standing there, on one leg now. Where the other leg used to be is loose, bloodless skin hanging down.

"Your turn now," says Slander. I can see the yellow membrane of his eardrum trembling. He nods excitedly at Idette, and I realize that this is the game he's making me play.

I stand up, take a step towards her. She smells like mothballs and sand after it rains. She looks at me all whites of her eyes, hands dripping orange goo on the snow. I want to puke.

"Play on!" says Slander.

I put my hand on her waist and she's cold and slick with mucus. I feel the blade of her hip under my palm. And as I hold it, it breaks loose and comes away all milky and wet in my hands, white, white and black. She staggers—hops— sideways, and then she collapses into the snow, all soft and insubstantial. Like my father.

Past her, Slander's eyes are shimmering, and my eyes are aching with the cold. And her hip bone in my hand feels like slime, and I let it go. I close my eyes, hold them shut with my other hand. When I open them, Slander is holding her hip bone in his hand.

"Yours?" he says to me.

My legs are numb past the knees, except for the violent sparks my nerves kick up from my feet. My body seizes my guts and gives them a hard squeeze. Comes up as a retch.

"Pay up," says Slander.

I put my hands in my pockets. All I have is the bottlecap. I feel Slander's wet hand open my fist, feel the points of the bottlecap, tacky with my blood, drop out of my palm; he doesn't cut me. It still hurts.

I know what's going to happen. I've known from the second I I opened my eyes this morning, from the second I saw him, from the moment I saw my dad in the hospital bed, from the second I put my suitcase down in the guest bedroom at Aunt Henny's house, from the moment I slid out of my mother's womb, from the moment my dad did to my mother what I did to Idette.

I'm too scared to move; I stop breathing, start praying: *Imago.* I stare off into the bare tree growing up beside the band shelter, forcing him to come.

And he does. With a violent burst of orange, he's there, sitting on a branch of the tree. The tree branch is still twanging under him.

"Imago," I say.

He isn't grinning, and he doesn't greet me. He only looks soberly from me to Slander, and he won't look back.

"Yes," says Slander. "I'm willing to forgive your debt, if…"

Here it is. He's giving me a chance.

"…your friend here will pay it for you," Slander finishes.

Imago won't look at me.

"And if he says 'no'?" I say.

The sound of Slander's laughter hurts me physically. He doesn't have to say it. Clever man; he knows. Of course Imago will do it if I ask him. He loves me.

"You won't hurt him?" I say. "I'll give him up if you promise not to—"

"You don't bargain with me, Danny," says Slander. "The terms are mine to make."

How can I? I think. But I have no choice.

"Was it worth it?" Slander's grin is so broad it nudges his eardrums.

I haven't seen Imago since. A month ago, my father went back to the institution. Aunt Henny doesn't talk about it. She doesn't talk much at all now, especially around me.

As I sit on my bed, writing in my journal, I feel something fingering the back of my neck. I launch myself out of bed, brushing off imagined spiders. But it's plaster dust that I find on my hand. The bedroom wall is now cracked from the ceiling to just above my pillow. And through the gap I see two long, white fingers and a black eye, watching me, reading my secrets. I hear his skin crease wetly as he smiles. As I watch, another lump of plaster breaks from the wall and falls free.

Pelly Medley

It was that indeterminate time between dawn and time to get up. The sunlight, stripped of color by the gray mist that hung over the island, still made its way through the curtains, making the cabin look like it was hung with sheets of drifting sand. Droplets of misty rain struck the windows; the wind was blowing strong today. Despite the sleeping bag and heavy blankets, Geoff felt cold. The heater, broken for a week, would not be replaced until Old Thomas came over from the mainland with new supplies. He was due to come today, but Geoff suspected the weather might keep him on the mainland.

The cabin vibrated as a gust of wind hit. Beyond the wind, Geoff could hear the sea colliding with the rocks. He got out of bed, wincing at the cold floor through his socks. The temperature on the island was a few degrees colder than on the mainland. The dampness was worse here too, this close to the sea.

Geoff made himself some coffee. As he sipped it, he pulled back the curtains from the north-facing window and confirmed what he'd feared. The sea was a pale lime gray, almost as though it were lit from within, thick, and capped with lines of white foam. Bits of cold rain, like grit, struck the window in gusts. Old Thomas would not be taking his boat out today, which meant Geoff would have to wait for new supplies from the mainland. He wrote in his logbook, 'May 26th: Inclement weather.'

Geoff donned his rain gear and went outside. He could not see the horizon; sky met sea in an opalescent haze. On clear days, when the coast was visible, it looked close enough to swim to, but distance was deceptive across water.

He climbed to the top of Pen Gwyntog. Already he was getting drenched with mist. The birds were keeping a low profile. *Don't humanize them,* he corrected himself.

He went down to the cove. The waves were jostling against the rocks, and there was no sign of Old Thomas. This part of the island always made him feel sad. Though it was now a wild bird preserve, the island had once been open to the public. He remembered coming here with his family on picnics. However, his memories of the island had diverged from the truth, idealizing it, making more of it than it was: A rock in the middle of nowhere. He wished that he could go back in time to find the island of his childhood. But he knew there was no such place.

It was time to go to work. He made his way to his regular vantage point overlooking the cliffs where he could see the black and white birds nestled in amongst the rocks. He lay near the edge, binoculars in hand, clipboard beside him, pinned under his elbow. He began his point counts, got into a routine tallying the birds in each randomly selected section of the cliff face. He marked each section on the clipboard as he finished them. He had developed a knack for working on his own, making comments into the voice-activated tape recorder in his jacket pocket. It was a peculiar state of total absorption that allowed the mind to wander.

And so he came to remember suddenly his bedroom at the summer cottage his parents rented when he was a child, and an antique brass birdcage hanging from a tall stand, and the budgie he'd kept inside it. A budgie called Medley.

The bird he was counting flapped and broke free of the cliff. Geoff felt the binoculars slip from his hand and they cart-wheeled down the cliffs.

"Shit," he said. They were his only pair.

He spent a frustrating hour trying to retrieve the binoculars. He was not equipped to attempt a climb down the cliffs, and he discovered, as he'd suspected, that the sea on that side of the island was very rough, and the cliffs weren't accessible from below either.

Eventually, soaked through, and bad-tempered, he gave up. He'd have to wait for Old Thomas and send a message to the university asking them to send him another pair. In the meantime, he'd have to make do with the telescope.

By the time he got back to the cabin, it was nearing dusk. He shut the cabin door, hard enough to make it vibrate, hard enough to surprise himself. He hadn't realized how angry he was.

He removed his boots, feeling a little shaken. When he straightened up, he discovered the real cause of his unease; someone had been in the cabin.

It was a subtle thing, nothing he could point to, but he had a clear mental picture of the way the cabin had looked when he'd left, and it had changed. His other coat was hanging askew on the hook. His pillow lay on the very edge of the bed.

He stood still and listened, heard the wind, the sound of rain flecking the windows, the floor beneath his feet creaking as he shifted his weight.

On his desk was a cardboard box that hadn't been there before. White letters on a black background spelled 'Imaginary Friends.' across the top. He vaguely remembered buying it from a souvenir shop, a converted terraced house with a pebble-dashed facade. A window displaying souvenir items, horse brasses, seashell artwork. A narrow interior, a flight of stairs to a small, slope-ceilinged room, sunlit but dim. He hadn't been able to make head or tails of the box's contents, and it had been lying under his bed for weeks.

Carefully, he lifted the lid from the box. It contained a heavy optical lens with a deep blue tinge. He held the lens up to the window. Through it, the sea looked blue-gray. Lining the bottom of the box a linen map lay unfurled—not much of a map, really, just an amoeba-shaped outline. The map had been altered since he had last seen it. Paths now crisscrossed the outline, and a little islet of rock had been inked in just inside the cove. Someone had printed "Nematode!" just above it and drawn in an arrow.

Arranged in a circle around the islet were brightly colored plastic board game tokens: A pink Easter egg, a blue seahorse, a green crocodile. And an orange one shaped like a pebble.

He peered around the cabin, still looking, hoping to find evidence that someone had been there. When Old Thomas was busy, he sometimes sent his son, Young Thomas to the island in his stead. Young Thomas had a sense of humor, perhaps more than was good for him.

Thomas?" he said. "Are you there?"

There was no answer.

Geoff went back to down to the cove, expecting to see Thomas' boat there. But even in the growing dusk, he could see that it was deserted.

Geoff searched the rest of the cabin, checking for anything else that might be missing or moved. He looked under the bed with his flashlight. Nothing else seemed to be out of place.

He sat at his desk and considered the bright plastic pieces. The orange one put him in mind of coloring sunsets with wax pencils, orange peel, those over-sweetened fruit drinks with no actual fruit in them, processed cheese, the crocheted curtains in the bedroom window at his grandmother's house, foxes, a bucket of beach sand leveled off at the top…

He picked the orange piece up. It was warm to the touch, like amber, orange like the color of hair. There had been a girl named Pelly living next to the seaside cottage his parents used to rent for the summer, a girl with hair that color. They'd been friends during the summers of his childhood. Before things had gotten complicated, before puberty, which had left him wondering what the point of it was. Looking back, he realized his best memories had happened before he'd acquired the hormone-tainted sophistication of adulthood. The old memories of his childhood remained, but the feelings had faded. He understood why: negative associations took longer to extinguish than positive ones. Maybe that was why people got sadder as they got older. Or maybe it was just him.

He set the orange piece on the windowsill, rolled up the map, put the lid on the box and slid it under his bed.

That night, the wind was blowing fiercely. If it kept up like this, Old Thomas wouldn't be coming tomorrow either. Geoff pulled the blankets up over his head to muffle the sound outside.

He woke up not knowing what time it was. It was dark. The cabin was shuddering; he heard the shriek of the wind outside, accompanied by the spray of flung waves hitting the rocks. There were no trees on the island, and the cabin was exposed to the elements. At some point, he thought, one big wave would wash right over the island, sweeping him and the cabin away with it. He stopped himself. He had to keep his mind off those thoughts or he'd go crazy.

He got up to transcribe his field notes from the tape recorder. He sat at his desk with the recorder beside him and pressed Play.

There was a hiss of silence then, a voice that was familiar, yet not. "Okay, Pelly, let's do another one. I'm standing on a beach in—no wait. Where am I?"

Geoff stopped the tape. That was his own voice, but he hadn't sounded like that since he was…since before his voice broke. He pressed Play again.

He heard someone breathing into the recorder. Then a girl's voice. "Ooooh! It's called, ehhhm… It's, ehhhm… It's—Nematode Norman's Holiday Camp for Sissies."

"Norman—can I call you 'Nematode'?" That was Geoff's voice again, the younger Geoff. "They say the treacle tart here tastes like phhht—" Stifled laughter. "…tastes like—" More giggling. The distorted sound of the Pause button being pressed and released. Then, in a serious voice this time, "—tastes like vomit. Do you have any comment?"

"Well," said a new voice. "Vomit-ish, I suppose."

Fizby, thought Geoff. That was Fizby's voice.

Stop. Rewind. Play.

The hiss of blank tape. He sped through the tape, searching for it, but the clip was gone.

Fizby had been his best friend years ago, curly brown hair except for a golf-ball-sized patch of blond behind his ear. Geoff knew now that that sort of thing was called a somatic mutation. Fizby used to claim it was his fairy blood showing through. Fizby who could run through a field of stinging nettles and come out on the other side without a single welt on him.

The next morning, he woke to the distinctive sound of crunching toast. He blinked the dim cabin into focus. The sunlight shone through the orange curtains, which had been beige when he'd gone to sleep, lit the kitchenette and a young woman perched with her bare feet up on the bench nibbling a triangle of toast globulous with marmalade.

She was all over with freckles, with a short upper lip and an upturned nose the tip of which bobbed when she chewed. Her eyes were mismatched, dark brown, light brown; her hair was orange, a burst of languorous curls. Her earrings were a pair of new pennies.

Geoff bolted upright in panic. When you've been alone for a long time, the sight of another person is not a welcome one; it is in a way, terrifying. Parts of you awake that had been slumbering, content.

"Morning," said the woman.

"But I don't have any marmalade," said Geoff stupidly.

"You do now, friend." The toast disappeared, and she took up a second triangle and picked up a wand running with honey. She drizzled it over the toast.

"What the hell are you doing here?" he said.

She crammed the entire slice into her mouth, shoving it home with her thumb. "Pelly Medley."

"Pardon?"

"My name's Pelly Medley."

"Medley?"

"Yeah, Medley. Medley, as in *everything*!" She spread her arms enthusiastically. "Everything all together, in one place. Me." She grinned. Her lips were covered in crumbs.

She sprang up and clutched his arm. Her fingers were warm and sticky. "Come. Outside, outside." She wasn't strong, but she was insistent. She dragged him out in his socks, outside onto the wet grass. The sun was out at last. She gripped his arm tighter and dragged him down to the cove.

"Hang on, Pelly! Wait a minute."

"Come on," she said and she pulled him right down the sand and into the water.

He staggered into the surf that swelled up around his knees. The next moment, she dove into an oncoming wave. He stood there, as the cold sea soaked into his clothes, waiting for her to resurface. She didn't. This was ludicrous, he thought. She couldn't have drowned. She must be having him on, had swum around the point under water.

He realized he was standing in the sea and it was not at all a comfortable place to be. He walked back to the shore, his socks squelching with every step. He called for her, went over the whole island, but she was gone.

He had reasoned it out by the time he got back to the cabin; he must have been dreaming. He'd sleepwalked in the past. That must be what had happened.

Except, when he got back to the cabin, he found a plate of crusts on the table. Bread crusts. He didn't keep bread. Bread went moldy in a matter of days, and he was often on the island for weeks between shipments of supplies from Old Thomas. Instead of bread, he spread margarine on vile thick cake-like things that clung to the inside of his mouth like sawdust.

He opened the cupboard and found it stocked with tins of peaches and apricots. And bread. Masses of it. A bottle of marmalade, unopened, and one of rowanberry jam. That wasn't right; with Old Thomas overdue to arrive, Geoff was down to the food he wouldn't normally look at, tinned mushrooms and sardines. Field work was bad for that. Geoff had already lost about ten pounds since the beginning of the field season.

That this cupboard was stocked with food—deleriously good, *proper food*—that was just impossible. Unless this girl, Pelly, had brought it with her. Or he was still sleepwalking and in a dream. He squeezed a loaf, felt the crust give under his thumb. Fresh. If you ate in a dream, did you wake up hungry?

Geoff sat down with a bread knife and devoured half a loaf. The stuff was soft, like it had been baked two minutes ago.

He was surprised how good he felt afterwards. It was time to do some work, count some birds.

It was human to make assumptions, to humanize what wasn't human, to trust one's instincts. Being a good scientist was a constant struggle against all of those things. Geoff prided himself on his methods; they were clean, objective and well founded. But today, he found that work had begun to feel like a chore. He didn't want to do it. He wanted to… He wanted to sit and watch the birds and for once, not have to think about what they were doing or why. So he wasn't being either objective or scientific when he went down to the cove.

At first, he thought it must be Old Thomas in his boat, the dark shadow moving on the water in the cove. But as he approached the beach he saw that it was mostly submerged, the water dark around it where it breached the surface. He was curious. He took his socks off, rolled up his trouser legs and waded out to it. By the time he reached it, the water was up to his knees. The shadow under the water looked like a spire of carboniferous limestone, the same kind of rock as on the coast. There had been no little island there yesterday. Maybe the tide was unusually low today. Maybe rocks sprang out of the sea without warning. Maybe he was losing his mind.

He heard a splash behind him, and he was hit in the back with a cascade of water. He turned. There was nothing there, but when he turned back to the rock, he saw someone perched on top of it, brandishing a microphone like a giant black lollipop in his face.

"Geoffrey, do you have any comments on these new developments on the island?" said the boy on the rock. He leaned down and stuck the microphone under Geoff's nose.

"Fizby?" said Geoff.

Fizby reached out and grasped the neck of Geoff's sweater and stuffed the microphone down it. Then he fell backwards into the water and vanished.

Geoff rummaged in his sweater for the microphone. He carried it with him as he slogged back to the island.

Pelly was sitting on the wooden shelf near the cabin's ceiling; Geoff had cleared off his data sheets to make room for her and had thrown a sleeping bag and his extra pillow up there for her. She was small enough that she fit in the space between ceiling and shelf. She was reading a book aloud to him, one he'd never read; he didn't know where she'd gotten it. It was so relaxing, being read to, that he started to doze off. He dreamt that he was standing in a hailstorm, and woke up with a jerk, feeling something striking his head. He opened his eyes to see Pelly leaning out from her bunk and dropping things onto him.

"Serves you right for falling asleep," she said.

"Have to work tomorrow," he murmured. It had been several days since he'd done any proper work.

Pelly snorted, as though unimpressed. She let her arm dangle over the edge of the bunk, holding another one of the game pieces loosely, as though she might drop it on him. Geoff reached up to take it, and she grasped his hand and didn't let go. He let her, even as the blood began to drain out of his arm and he got pins and needles in his fingers.

He did not know how to take her. As interloper, guest, wayward girl, friend…? On one thing he was clear; whatever he felt it wasn't lust, nor even its second cousin.

As he dozed off, he remembered what had happened to his budgie, Medley. His parents had buried her in the sand down at the beach, in the cardboard box she'd come home in from the pet store. She hadn't lasted the summer.

He woke feeling a peculiar species of wrongness, the feeling of having slept well and long, through something very important. He looked at his watch. Three PM. He'd gone to bed at nine PM.

He got out of bed. The plywood shelf above the bed was crammed tight with his logbooks. A layer of dust lay on top of them. He opened the cupboard and found stacks of dull, gray sardine tins.

He opened his logbook. His last entry was May 25th. He didn't know what day it was today. But the weather was cold, the sky murky, the sea more unruly than usual.

Geoff had a flare gun which he could fire off in an emergency, but this wasn't an emergency. He could picture the distress call: 'Have run out of tinned peaches. Please bring more!'

He went down to the cove. On the way, he tripped and stumbled over his own feet. No, not his own feet…the corner of a white tablecloth spread out over the grass. Set on the tablecloth were three white plates. And food, real food, in bold colors: chocolate éclairs, strawberries, mandarin orange segments.…

"Treacle tart?" said Fizby holding out a wedge to him, balanced on a pie-cutter. "Tastes a little vomit-ish, but you get used to it."

Pelly was sitting across from Fizby drinking ginger beer straight from the bottle. She shoved a bottle at Geoff. It was cold, with condensation beading on the outside. What was this? And how did he find himself sitting on the grass between them, drinking this stuff that made the back of his nose itch it was so strong, eating sandwiches with real squashy bread and fending off wedges of treacle tart?

And how was it he found himself lying on his back watching the birds in the sky for hours before he realized he hadn't even noticed which ones were banded? He had seen them as work for so long that he had forgotten how beautiful they were. He had learned his profession so that someone would pay him to do what he loved. Only it had become something he did for pay, and love—real love—had gone by the way.

At what point in his life had love come to mean sex? When had his toys become tools? What he had been doing for years now was to capture in numbers and models, what came to him now openly here. He had overlooked it, or perhaps, been looking too hard when he only had to sit back and see. It wasn't that difficult.

As he watched the birds, they became agitated, wheeling around overhead and whistling, flying in circles, crossing each other's flight paths, weaving in and out. He sat up. The disturbance was centered on Pen Gwyntog. Pelly was sitting there, cross-legged with something on her lap. As he came up behind her, he saw flashing colors. She was holding out her fingers with a cat's cradle of some iridescent floss stretched between them. She threaded her fingers one way and another, turned and twisted and the patterns shimmered and fluttered between her palms, magenta, blue, orange.

"What are you doing?" he asked.

"Flying the birds," she said.

Feeling like he'd missed something, he went back to the cabin. He didn't know what day it was. Old Thomas still hadn't come. Geoff looked out through the cabin window. The glass was tinged with blue. He still could not see the coast. He had not seen the coast for as long as he could remember.

Old Thomas wasn't coming. There was no Old Thomas, no Young Thomas, no mainland, no nothing. Just this.

Geoff went back outside to play catch with Pelly and Fizby and the birds.

Bluecoat Jack

Published in *TEXT: UR—The New Book of Masks*, 2007.
Honorable Mention, *Year's Best Fantasy & Horror*, 2008.

Things started to fall apart about two months ago when I picked up the new conduit at the Grayhound Bus Terminal. Weyland, who handed him off to me, told me this one's name was Jack. That was what he was calling him. It's all bogus. Weyland isn't his real name and Henry isn't mine, but we had to call each other something, and no one wanted to remember who they used to be.

After handing Jack off to me, Weyland booked it out the door like he needed to be somewhere, yesterday, leaving me with my pickup—Jack. He was the youngest conduit I'd ever seen. He looked about fifteen, lounging in the plastic bus station chair with his coat on. Everything looked hard and blaring under those bus terminal lights, and that blue coat of his was just seething with color.

We had a half-hour wait for our bus. "Stay there," I told him, and I picked up a coffee from the stand near the ticket wickets, keeping an eye on him the whole time. He stayed in that awkward, half-reclining slouch almost sliding off his chair. I hoped he wasn't getting sick; I didn't feel like holding his head while he puked up whatever Weyland had fed him.

I brought back the coffee and sat down opposite him, had a good look at him. Though it was hot in the terminal, his coat was closed to his throat. Pulled closed —the buttons were missing. His hair was blonde, curly, longer than it needed to be, falling down past his eyes, hiding his expression, if he even had one. Not all of them did by the time I got them. His knees were the most expressive thing about him, alternately gaping and pressing the palms of his hands together between them. I sipped my coffee and watched him doing nothing like I couldn't get enough of it.

Five minutes before departure, our bus was called. There's something about the smell of diesel exhaust that reminds me of wet Sunday evenings and dying. I don't like to breathe it, and I avoid it as much as I can, even though this time it meant we nearly missed our bus.

And maybe it was because it was after midnight, or because I'd had too much coffee, but the sound of the bus driver tearing Jack's ticket was like a short scream and so blinding white it looked in his hand. Jack didn't have a bag with him, hadn't asked me what my name was, where I was taking him. There was that resignation in him… and a kind of nobility.

I took Jack to the back of the bus and sat him by the window. The bus pulled out not long after. I switched off the overhead lights and watched Jack watch the street-lit rain streaking the window. We were necessarily closer than I normally like to get to another person. My eyes started to kill, so I closed them, sitting up extra tall to keep myself awake. I could hear him breathing next to me, slow and deep.

I nearly slept through the stop, despite the coffee. As the bus lurched to a stop outside the motel, I touched his arm with the pen I carried. The material of his coat was so soft the pen sank into it like a blown cat-tail. Wool, maybe. Expensive wool. Must be stolen, I thought. Conduits didn't have money.

Outside, the air smelled cold. It was two AM and we were the only ones on the street. I fished out the motel keycard. The room was humid, smelt of damp concrete. The carpet was greasy beneath my feet. Everything was where I'd left it, but I checked anyway, under the bed, outside the patio door. I didn't let him use the bathroom until I'd made sure the shower was clear, even then, I made him leave the door open.

After Jack came out of the bathroom, he curled up on the bed with his shoes and his coat still on, pulled the pillow into the crook of his arm and hugged it. He closed his eyes.

The coffee was still affecting me; I couldn't sleep. I went to the patio door, held the curtains back and looked out across the parking lot—there were only two cars, and tote windows of the other rooms were dark. Jack sounded asleep, the sleep of the untroubled, the innocent. I picked up the ice bucket and went down the hallway to fill it from the machine. The rattle in the plastic bucket sounded like bombs going off. The feel of the plastic bucket in my hand, ice against my knuckles, my whole body juddered with each step. My feet seemed very far beneath me and insubstantial. I slipped the keycard into the lock and let myself back in.

He was lying in exactly the same position, but he looked smaller; maybe it was the way he was curled up around that pillow. He looked terribly young, eyes closed in the glow of the bedside lamp. Looking at him I felt a little strange, older suddenly.

I set the ice bucket on the table gently and sat on the other bed, watching him. I sat there for a long time, thinking of a lot of things, like how long it had been since anyone had trusted me enough to fall asleep that close to me, someone who hadn't wanted anything from me.

Suddenly I wanted with all my heart to protect this kid from everything outside this room, from everything in the world, everything that could possibly damage him more than he obviously had been. But you have a job to do, I thought. Keep him safe until Spring needs him. After that, it's out of your hands.

I turned off the lamp and lay there listening to him breathe. It wasn't a conscious decision to stay awake. We were safe; no one had followed us here. But I wanted to be aware of every moment as it passed, because we were at a temporary peace, and I knew it wouldn't last.

I eventually encountered something like sleep, a series of troubled wanderings through gray worlds that weren't quite dreams and weren't quite nothing. Like wandering in the cloudland on a thundery day.

I was a wreck by morning. When I glimpsed myself in the mirror, I had a pretty good idea what I was going to look like dead. Jack looked maybe a little more rumpled, a little less detached than last night.

"I'll back the car up to the entrance once I've settled the bill," I said. "Don't come out until I pull up."

It was a hell of an odd morning. I paid the bill, feeling like the first time out of bed after the flu. The air was sharp, and next to the motel the tulips lay in their beds, fresh-frozen.

Jack's thick coat looked appropriate today. Good, less chance people would take notice of him. For the same reason, we couldn't stop for a meal; in small towns like this, people noticed strangers, and eating at a restaurant would give them time to do exactly that. Look, mum. Cityfolk.

By the time we got back to my house it was daylight. I pulled the car into the garage and hustled Jack up the path to the back of the house. It's an old bungalow in a street of older and better houses. Behind the garage and down a ravine run the train tracks. Close enough that the house rattles when a train goes by. Couldn't keep anything on the windowsills. A poor thing, but mine own—well, it was Spring's actually, but it came with the job.

It wasn't ideal bringing Jack in while it was light out and the neighbors could potentially see him, so I made sure I was quick getting him inside.

"You hungry?" I asked.

He looked over his shoulder at me. "No," he said, really quiet.

I showed him to the spare bedroom. Nothing fancy—just a bed by the wall, an empty shelf above it and a closet with no hangers. I left him there to sort himself out.

I didn't know where they came from—the conduits—and I never asked. All I knew was the way Spring treated them, there was no way they had got a home to go back to. None of them ever asked me if they could use my phone. Clearly, they had no one to call, no one who missed them.

I used to wonder if that was part of the reason they made such good conduits. But then it occurred to me that people who had no one who cared about them weren't worth as much as the ones who did, and maybe it was easier for Spring and her cronies to take people like that and do what they did to them.

When I first met Spring I'd had ambitions of learning her craft, the art of creating beautiful things from the unwanted, exploiting the soul's inner beauty. My disillusionment happened softly and slowly, until one day I woke up and realized I was nothing but Spring's lackey. But by then, I couldn't imagine a life other than this one I already had. I ought to be happy with it, because god knew, other people were much worse off than me.

The time when I used to try and figure out what made the conduits special was long past. It was no longer a glorious pursuit of artistic perfection. It was just a job.

The conduits were all different. I wouldn't say there was a typical 'type.' You couldn't use the same approach with all of them either. You had to be flexible, adaptable. I was that, which was one of the reasons Spring liked to use me. I was also discreet. It's easy to be discreet, when you have no one to tell, no one real, anyway.

The one before Jack wouldn't shut up. Talked in his sleep too. About nothing. The one before that liked to take things apart, took the legs off my kitchen table and the door off the fridge. The one before that was all twitchy, gave me the creeps having him in the house. Before that was an eighteen-year-old druggie with a cold. Coughed and sneezed the whole time, sprayed mucus everywhere.

I kept them until Spring was ready to see them. Being a caretaker involved a lot of waiting. With Jack, she kept me waiting longer than usual. But finally, she called.

I brought him to Spring's at six PM that first time, parked the car in a side street I wasn't supposed to park in, hopped out and unlocked the back door to the building. Spring shared a back door with a firm of lawyers; none of them used that door very often. It was quiet in the hallway. I hustled Jack into the building and up the stairs. There was a brief moment when I saw a silhouette through the frosted glass in an office door, but I was practically shoving Jack up the stairs and into Spring's apartment at that point.

"Stay there. Don't touch anything," I said. "Wait for me." Then I ran back downstairs to move my car before it got towed.

When I'd done that, I came back to Spring's place through the front door this time. Spring's loft apartment was full of the kind of things that catch your eyes and hold them tight, that challenge you to figure them out. Spring told me a beautiful face has the same effect, but I wouldn't know. All the things in Spring's loft were beautiful. Her studio motto is, 'Turning Aspects into Art.' The logo, in a stained glass panel in the skylight, is a monarch caterpillar with a butterfly above it.

There were new things in Spring's apartment every time I came. Some of them she sold for lucrative prices to wealthy clients, some of them she kept. The loft was lit up with colors, bright glass, plastic, prismatic, animated figures, three-dimensional pictures within pictures, a grandfather clock with wind chimes inside, two dragon kites sixteen feet long dogfighting in the rafters. Little flickering black things like confused moths persisted in the corners, remnants of Spring's less successful bouts with a conduit. The clients who paid so handsomely for Spring's art probably didn't trouble themselves about where it come from.

Jack took no notice of any of it; he was standing by the picture window with his back to me looking out at the city. Spring had tried to tempt me with money, her body, her art, but what had ultimately seduced me was the view of the city from her loft. When I saw it like that, never mind its stinking gutters cluttered with the viscera of audio cassettes, the pavements embossed with blackened gum, the backed-up sewers, the harbor with its boats rotting out from under them, the egg-shattering noise of the trains, the narrow, stifling streets. From this vantage, everything looked right; everything was where it ought to be, lights all shining along the waterfront. I think Jack must have thought so too. He had this wistful expression. He understands, I thought, and I felt a glimmer of elation. And then Spring came in.

There was nothing soft about her, her hair, like a tangle of brass springs, the sharp seam of her trousers where they hung from the points of her knees, her barbed wire bracelets. When she smiled, her lips were like the edges of a cut.

"Well?" said Spring, looking at Jack. I hated that wanting look she had.

Jack turned from the window, regarding her calmly. He shook his head.

"You don't have a choice," she said. "If I have to force you, I will."

"Spring…" I said.

"Make yourself scarce, Henry," she said.

I left Jack and went up to the roof, letting the door slam behind me, I was in that kind of a mood where I wanted to make noise. The pigeons stirred, but none of them took flight. It was too late, too dark despite the urban twilight. I sat down on a cinder block and put a foot up on the corner of the roof garden. Across from me sat Erisel, my stone lioness.

I'd had a soft spot for stone lions ever since I was little. My kid brother Mick and I used to believe they came alive under moonlight. Some nights we stayed awake peering through the bedroom window at the rustling hedge in our front yard, wondering if lions could break through glass.

Erisel looked the part. She wasn't one of those down-sized, coarse-cut things that pretentious suburbanites stuck on their lawns. She was a library lioness, and sometimes she was the only thing that kept me going.

They have a term for what happens to caretakers: compassion fatigue. Most caretakers succumb to it, become drunks or druggies. Erisel was why I could handle working as a caretaker without resorting to alcohol, drugs or the other things caretakers ended up doing. For a while I'd assumed Spring had stolen this one from the steps of the public library and brought her here with the help of her shit-disturbing Engineer friends. But when Spring found me up on her roof and asked me who I was talking to, and she looked through Erisel like she wasn't there, I realized that maybe what I was doing wasn't too healthy either, but when your illusions give you comfort, it's hard to let them go.

"A bald man and a lady in a pink coat walked along the sidewalk earlier tonight," said Erisel. "I could have dropped one of these cinder blocks on their heads if I'd wanted."

"You get bored too easily," I said.

"A lifetime of guarding books, of looking noble and dignified. It gets to you. Are you all right?"

"Why shouldn't I be?"

"You seem as though someone broke your heart, that's all."

"The day someone breaks my heart—" I protested.

"Is the day I lie down with a lamb." I heard her laugh in the roar of the wind over the rooftops.

Some time afterward I went back downstairs. I avoided looking around Spring's apartment, but something blue caught my eye. In a ceramic candy dish on the kitchen table was a button, the size of my thumbnail, smooth, transparent blue glass, chipped on the rim. It was still warm. When I held it to the light a flickering animation appeared inside, the way light plays on the ceiling above a swimming pool. Then I realized that what I was seeing was private, not mine to see. The kind of thing someone gives you if you're very lucky, or worthy. Not the kind of thing you just take.

"Jackpot," said Spring. I could hear her smirking. "Get him out of here, would you, Henry?"

I took Jack home. It was early, before dawn. I could see him suffering, but I couldn't do anything for him. Except leave him alone. I left him in his room and shut the door. Then I went to the living room, sat and stared at the street through my window, holding my hands over my ears, because the door wasn't muffling his sobs and what wood couldn't do, maybe flesh could.

After three visits to Spring, most of the conduits were done. A few hung on for four. Some were finished after two. The light went out of their eyes. Not a butterfly after all, but a dried up cocoon. Then I would take them back to Weyland. I don't know what he did with them.

I didn't know how many times Jack had been used before he came to me. Once at least, I think. So he had maybe two more visits left in him, at worst, one.

The waiting was the worst part. No, the worst part is when the phone rings at three AM, and I wake up like someone yanked on my spinal cord. It was that deep inside, Spring's hold on me.

"Yeah?" I said.

"Bring him over," said Spring.

I switched off the phone, set it on the floor beside the bed. It had now become inevitable, wasn't my problem.

Jack was bundled up on the bed, coat still on. I shook him awake. He lay there with his elbow across his face, like he thought I was going to hit him. I pulled on my boots at the door, walked back to his bed. "Up. Now." Nudge in the ribs, or whatever pillow-filling passed for them in his chest. He rolled off the bed onto the floor, got up like an old man.

Every caretaker found a way to cope; some ways were universal. One of them is, when you're into the homestretch, when it's almost over, you never look them in the eyes. Eye contact makes a connection, like joining live wires. You can burn yourself out doing it.

It's easier to distance yourself if you're a little rough with them near the end. I hauled Jack out the door by the elbow, shoving him onto the pathway. I shoved him a couple more times on the way to the car, hard enough to make him stumble.

At three AM there was no one on the streets apart from taxis.

"I can't," he said. "Not again. Don't make me, please."

"Shut up," I said. And thank God, he did.

I could see Spring watching us from the lit window of her loft as we pulled up.

I went inside, walked straight up to Spring. "Don't push him," I said. "He's going to fall apart."

"Into oh, what pretty pieces," she said.

I felt a sudden, unexpected surge of anger.

She must have sensed it. "Don't get attached," she told me. "He's not a velveteen rabbit."

"What's that supposed to mean?"

"He's not real. You can't make him real by caring."

"Stop trying to make this about me."

She glanced skyward, her barbed-wire bangles sliding down her wrist. "It's not about you, you self-obsessed idiot. It's business."

I went up to the roof and sat on the cinderblock next to Erisel. I put my arm around her, held her, stroked the back of her ear. She was cold, but I could feel her anger, so powerful, I felt it, even though she wasn't really there, and I was leaning on nothing but air and wishful thinking.

You learn to live a certain way, to avoid a certain kind of situation. You get so good at it that no one realizes what you're doing, even you. Years pass, until at some point, someone remarks that hey, you've never had a girlfriend, have you, sport? Isn't that odd? Despite set-ups from your well-meaning family, despite awkward situations with aggressive girls who put their hands on you because you don't have the balls to tell them to back off, or the heart to tell the nice girls that you don't care and never could. Then people start suggesting that you're gay, and you think, well, maybe I am. Except the first time a guy makes a pass at you and you let him, you puke and get the shakes whenever you think about it afterward. So, maybe you're not gay after all. You don't know what you are. If it even has a name. And instead of trying to deny what you are, you exploit it; you find an occupation where not caring about people is an asset. Where keeping your hands off them is considered professional, where no one expects more of you than you're willing to give. You were born to be a caretaker—there's nothing else out there for you but this. You can't walk away from it; it's who you are.

After his second session with Spring, Jack was in a bad way. He could walk around without hitting walls, sit down when I told him to, but that was it. I was babysitting a catatonic. I'd seen that look before. He might pick up, recover a little, but one more trip to Spring and he'd be finished. Then it would be back on the bus again to meet Weyland, watching the gray streets slide by, breathing stale air that had lived in a hundred smokers' lungs. I always think of grit and the breathless state of imminent illness whenever I think of Weyland. The thought of seeing him again so soon was more than I could take.

I went to bed, left Jack sitting on the couch—he wouldn't lie down, and I didn't have it in me to make him do what he didn't want to. When

I woke up in the middle of the night to get a glass of milk, he was still sitting there, except now there was a pad of paper on the table with a pen next to it. The page was covered in sloppy handwriting. It said: ON SCEDULE ON SCEDULE ON SCEDULE ON SCEDULE

A whole page of it.

I went back to my bedroom and sat on the bed.

Why this one? Fifty others, at least, had passed through my hands. I hadn't let myself care about any of them. Was it Jack or the guilt from all those others? Each time one went through, I felt a little bit of guilt, not much, a little, like throwing away a piece of litter. But it never went away; it added up, and each time the thought: What if I stop now? was a little more insistent. No, Henry, you have it too good to throw this away. You're living the only life you can, in the only place you fit in.

Except suddenly you find yourself caring about someone so much that you're willing to face a situation so they don't have to. You tell yourself to put that feeling away, but you're already so full of the things you're hiding from yourself that there's nowhere left to put it.

I thought about basic human needs and how many of them I'd been needing and for how long, things I used to have, things I thought I'd never have again.

I thought about dying, and how it couldn't be much worse than this.

Spring had me snug in her pocket. The house belonged to her. She gave me money—enough to live on, a little extra sometimes. I'd been putting aside the extra over the years, but it wouldn't be enough to get Jack and me very far. We couldn't run. If we tried to leave, they'd find us.

Spring sat at her kitchen table, clasping her hands over her knees, looking at me. "What did you say?"

"Take me instead," I said.

"Why?"

"Because I can handle it."

"Clearly you can't or you wouldn't be offering to take his place. You don't know what you're saying."

"I know exactly what I'm offering. Where do you think I've been for the past ten years?!" I was worried she'd refuse because she didn't think I had the goods; I was a caretaker, not a conduit.

She pinched her earlobe and played with it between her fingers. "I had plans for you," she said. "Other plans."

"I have plans for me," I said.

"Not when I'm finished," she said.

I packed my stuff. Didn't know what I'd need or how long I'd be gone, but that wasn't what I was worrying about. I bought groceries—cans, bottles, instant soup packets. Enough to last a while. I packed the freezer tight with boxed food. I tried not to dwell on whether he'd know what to do with any of it, whether he even knew how to cook. Jack sat watching me, like it had nothing to do with him. He looked sad. Part of me was angry that he didn't seem to realize what it all meant, what I was doing for him.

When I was done, I put a plate in front of him. "I made you a sandwich."

He didn't even look at it.

"Help yourself to the food. You should be all set for a while."

He just looked at me and blinked, and I started to realize then that he probably didn't even know how to make ice cubes, and I was leaving him here alone. I thought about him going outside in that coat without buttons, and I unzipped my jacket; I'd saved up and bought a good warm one. I put it over the back of his chair. "If you go out, wear this, okay? And pull the hood up."

W orrying about Jack stopped me worrying about Spring's plans for me, until the second she pulled open her door to let me in. All cool, all business, like we'd never really talked, like she'd never gotten drunk and made a pass at me one night on her roof.

No, I recognized that demeanor, because I'd adopted it too. It was the classic pull-back, the detachment you assume with the conduits before they're about to be used.

But I was a volunteer; I had motivation. It was back in my house blinking at my walls, staring out my window, and very probably going hungry.

Spring sent me upstairs. The upper floor in her loft was simply a platform that extended over a quarter of the ceiling. It wasn't walled off and with the open plan, if you were standing across the room from it on the main level, you could see some of what was up there. You had to climb a ladder to get to it. At the top, I could feel all the warm air collecting under the skylight. There was a futon opened up on the floor with some new sheets on it. Fresh-out-of-the-package new.

She told me to take off my clothes. I wondered if she'd made Jack do that, and was that why he was so fucked up afterwards. I was dreading that she was going to touch me. I knew she'd never forgiven me for rejecting her advances that night.

But Spring's idea of revenge was more subtle than simply putting her hands on me.

"Lie down," she said.

I did, but when she leaned over me, I said, "Don't touch me."

"You're not calling the shots any more, sport," she said.

I looked up at the skylight, at the monarch butterfly in the glass.

I'd never watched her work before; I didn't know her technique. As it happened, it was worse than physical intimacy.

From where I lay, I saw her pull what looked like a sketchpad from under the bed. She opened it, and all the pages inside were black. As she flipped through, I saw that they weren't made of paper, but some flakey stuff, like mica, that powdered her palms. It looked familiar, and I realized it was the same stuff those little flitting shadows in the rafters were made of. She found a page she liked, pulled it out and laid it on my chest. It was soft and cold, and I wanted it off me.

"Close your eyes," she said.

I did, but I watched her between my lids.

"What do you see?" she said.

The mica fluttered on my chest, like snowflakes landing and though my eyes were half-open, I saw it clearly.

A playground. Swings. She's watching. Who? I didn't want to go back, but there I was, like I'd never left. Maybe part of me never really had, that day at the playground with Mick, watching him on the slide. I felt the swing hitch under me, but it wasn't till after I fell that I realized someone had given me a good kick while the swing was in mid-air, not till it was too late that I realized why. All I knew then was that when the frozen ground hit me sideways something broke inside my body, like a toy that's been left out in the rain and then stepped on, and all I could do was watch while the man in the gray sweater stepped over me and picked

Mick up and took him away. Look after your little brother, my mother told me as she left to talk to her friends. I was always looking after Mick because no one else would. My parents didn't say it, but he'd been a mistake. They hadn't wanted another kid. Mick was very young, but I think even he knew they didn't want him. But that man in gray had, the one who kicked me off the swing so I couldn't run and tell anyone. I could see him now, plain as day. Old man, ugly thick sweater, a look in his eyes like he owned the world, like nothing could stop him. I had wanted so much to stop him, to protect Mick from him. I wanted him to take me instead. Approach him, said Spring. I struggled, as I had that day, in futility. Then I felt her hands on me, lifting me up, lending me the power to act. I had never hated anyone so much as that man and now after so long, I could stop him, do what I wanted to him. I was powerful, enraged, and I launched myself across the playground. I would have had him in three bounds. Then—

Surrender her, said Spring.

No. One more leap and I'll have him down.

Now! she said.

I felt that stuff melting on my skin, entering me, and I felt the broken things inside me shifting, and pain. You know that feeling, like you've got steel wool packed under your cheekbones, that seething metal tang you taste when you're about to pass out? The second before I closed on that man, just before I reached him, I felt it throttle me, and out I went.

I open my eyes. My body feels like it's been turned inside out and rolled in sand, and I can't move. I make some kind of noise, don't know what I'm trying to say. I hear Spring's voice below. "You compartmentalize well," she says. "You made it easy." I hear her climbing the ladder. "You surprised me. I never guessed you had such a fierce maternal instinct. You, a grown man." She puts a glass of water on the floor beside me. "You can go when you're ready."

My body won't let me move. I doze… wake up. This time I can move. I drink the warm, dusty water, get dressed, creep down the ladder, clinging to it like it's made of rope not pine. Spring's sitting cross-legged on her bean bag chair with a teacup in her hand. "I didn't know you had a brother," she says. She takes a sip of her tea. I hear her swallow. "You want to see it, you can. I put it in the spare room."

I go up to the roof instead. It's cold, breath-misty cold, and dark. I don't know how long I've been here, feels like years. The roof is empty, covered in fine grit. I shuffle around, looking for something, but I don't know what. Nothing's here, but it feels like there should be. I'm lonely and doing this isn't helping. I go back downstairs. Spring's sitting on the bean bag chair with a plate of oysters on her lap. I go to the kitchen, take her keychain off the table. Then I go to the spare room.

"I thought you'd want to see it," she says.

The room isn't set up for human guests. It's full of things, but I don't have to guess which one she took from me.

My real name isn't Henry. It's what people call me now, but I was named Leonard after my grandfather. My brother, Mick, called me Leo.

I unlock the padlock on her cage. She's full of rage, and she frightens me. I take the padlock off. As soon as she brushes against it, the door will open easily. She isn't mine any more, and she'll hurt me if I stay.

I leave the spare bedroom, return Spring's keys to the table. Before I go, I take the button out of the ceramic candy dish on the table. Then I go home.

When I get there, Jack is sitting on the couch, like he hasn't so much as blinked since I left. I wonder why he's still here. I go and put the button on his knee, the little glass button with the shifting vista inside. He stares and stares, but the life in his eyes is gone.

A Sip from the Cup of Enlightenment

Published in *Polyphony 7*.

Anders had been teaching at the Gwyntog school for nearly a month before discovering the red hands in one of the outbuildings on the school grounds. The school was situated on the Gwyntog Coast, far enough inland to be out of sight of the sea, but close enough to shore that the north-facing windows of Anders' lodgings were often flecked by sea spray during the violent autumn storms typical in that part of the world. The wind kept Anders awake. Shaka Pask, the Divinity Lecturer, assured him that he would get used to it in time.

On this particular afternoon, Anders sat in his study, preparing the week's lessons. He was becoming increasingly uncomfortable with the duties his job entailed. The subject Anders taught was purportedly History. Anders' training was in English Literature. However, during the job interview, the dean of the Gwyntog School had explained to him that they were somewhat short-staffed and in need of a temporary History instructor. He had given Anders the impression that they were desperate to fill the position. The job included free accommodation in one of the school's many houses. Anders had troubles of his own in England, troubles he was eager to leave behind. He had therefore pretended that he was perfectly comfortable teaching History. And he might have been, had it been the normal sort of history.

Anders flicked his pen down in the crease of the lessons book. Beside him lay the open text he had been studying, left behind by the previous History lecturer: *A History of the Gwyntog Coast, the Congaree Marches and Isle Itself: Hanson's Modern English Edition.*

The passage he had been studying read: "*...and the Oracle went into the Tower at Black Tor and had congress with the dragon therein and emerged with the gift of prophecy, saying, 'You shall take your sins and* *set them under the Bridge for all to see, and you will pray until the river runs clear and you will know redemption…* "

"You must be joking," Anders muttered.

Perhaps it was less preposterous in the original language. If they'd called the subject Mythology it would have been one thing, but he was teaching it as local history, as Truth. Dragons and prophets. Where was Gwyntog when the rest of the world was turning?

Anders had had enough. He scraped back his wooden chair. Through the window of his study, he saw that the sun lit the lawn between the students' dormitories and the teachers' lodgings. Winter was coming on; he ought to enjoy the weather before the cold set in. And a walk might help shake off his uneasiness.

He wasn't the only one enjoying the day. Wandering along the river, he saw two teams of six boys, seniors by the looks of them, racing along the muddy bank in the school's yellow and gray jerseys.

Shorey ambled past him with his elderly dog, and at the edge of the pitch, the Reckoner was standing with his red gloves on like a Santa Claus dispensing wisdom instead of presents. *No thanks,* thought Anders, walking on. Oblivious to where he was going, he passed the boathouse and the boys' dormitories, and by the time he finally became aware of his surroundings, he had no idea where he was.

The pathway in front of him ended in a close—a semicircle of old buildings standing in a state of neglect with the trees pressing in around them, because presumably no one had been cutting them back. The buildings were all five-story-high, brick affairs with stone archways above their doors. They had a more formal feel to them than the dormitories or the tutors' lodgings nearer the school.

Intrigued, Anders went to the closest one. Cut into the stone archway above the door was the word, *Sipdraft.* The windows were smoked glass, rippled, obscured with dust. The lowest ones were situated well above Anders' head—too high for him to look through. He tried the door and found it locked. He had been given a myriad of pocket-cluttering keys when he had arrived at the school. One for the chapel, at least three for his own house; he still hadn't discovered what they were all for. He tried each of them in this lock, but none would fit.

He went to the other buildings in turn: *Eden, Alydar, Aven,* and *Verdegris.* The names looked oddly familiar.

Verdegris's lock had been sprung. Pushing the door inward he heard the whisper of old paper and caught the glimmer of cigarette smoke.

The hall echoed, full of sunlight shining through the smoked windows. In one of the rooms on the main floor, he discovered several large packing crates, the wooden boards stamped in a language he didn't recognize. The crates were old and smelt of mildew. Dust coated his palms like felt when he touched one of them. It was five feet high, large enough to house a grand piano and impossible to shift or open with his bare hands. He gave up and found the stairs.

This was another proposition entirely. It was a pity, he thought, that this building had fallen into disuse. The architect had obviously had a gift for manipulating light and exploiting refraction. The stairs spiraled upward around a hollow glass column running from the basement to the cupolaed ceiling sixty feet above. Inside the column on shelves, stood various unidentifiable objects in blown glass, tarnished metal and dark wood, arranged to catch the light. It put him in mind of the display cases in the medical building at his college, curiosities in jars. Aesthetic grotesque. The morbid seduction of the eyes.

On the fifth and highest level, he rounded the stairs and came upon the last display. The display case ended three feet above his head and ten feet below the cupolaed ceiling. The sun, directly overhead now, shot rays refracted into indigos, reds and yellows upon a pair of skeletal hands. These had been mounted on an ebony base, supported by cunningly hidden wires to simulate a lifelike pose. The hands were cupped, holding a thick glass vessel. The bones of the hand were colored the red of bitter cherry, but they looked entirely real.

Anders leaned over the stair railing to look more closely. The wrist bones were glued and fitted together like a Chinese ivory puzzle. As he stared at the hands, the shadows beneath them lengthened. The sun was crossing the sky. Anders shook himself out of his reverie. It was getting late. He descended the stairs and found his way back to his lodgings where his books awaited him.

But that evening as he resumed his preparation for the next day's lesson, he could not put the hands from his mind. He pictured them as they must look in the dim gallery, holding that dull glass vessel as though it were the most precious thing on Earth.

The next day, and those that followed, the hands continued to haunt him. He caught himself dreaming about them during chapel services, at night as he tried to sleep through the gusting wind, and once, in the middle of a lesson, he was brought abruptly out of a reverie to see his students staring at him, perplexed. It took him a moment to realize that one of them had just asked him a question. Bilbury, one of the brighter and more outspoken students.

"Pardon?" said Anders.

"Was the Oracle a manifestation of God, Sir?" Bilbury asked.

"What?"

"Except, you just told us that the Oracles were omniscient. If they knew everything, what else could they have been?"

"The Oracles were the *conduits* of God," said one of the other boys. "Or were you asleep when Shaka Pask taught us that?"

"Shut up, both of you!" Anders snapped. "This is History, not fucking Divinity!"

The boys collectively flinched in shock.

"Class dismissed," said Anders, and he left the room.

Shaka Pask, the Divinity lecturer, lived in an apartment in the boys' dormitory. That was where Anders found him.

"May I come in?" said Anders.

"Most certainly," said Pask.

Anders settled himself onto the old settee in Pask's sitting room. He regarded Pask while deciding how to begin. Pask was no more than a few years older than Anders, and as the youngest member on staff, Anders felt more affinity towards him than any of the other lecturers. Pask went about in a habitually disheveled state, usually unshaven, and wore a deceptively sleepy expression.

Anders took a deep breath. "The dean's just had a go at me for my behavior in lesson the other day."

"I heard," said Pask.

"I just wanted to ask you not to…" Anders fidgeted with his shirt cuff.

"Not to what?"

"I'd appreciate it if you wouldn't put ideas into the boys' heads regarding the local history. They ask me these questions, and it's not my area." Anders heard the edge in his own voice and realized he was angry. "It's not my business to sort that out."

"To sort what out, exactly?" said Pask calmly.

"God. Religion."

"Oh. That nonsense," said Pask.

Anders blinked. "You teach Divinity, and you're not a believer?"

"The more I teach it, the less I believe in it."

"How can you teach what you don't believe?" said Anders.

"I just think of it as imparting knowledge. That's all it is."

"But doesn't the truth matter here?"

Pask laughed. "You and I deal in the pursuit of Knowledge, not the pursuit of Truth."

"What's the damned difference?" said Anders.

"Truth requires faith. Knowledge does not. Faith isn't our concern. That is the province of the Reckoner."

"I don't understand the point of the Reckoner," said Anders. "I don't understand your religion at all."

"You were born and raised abroad, and it shows," said Pask. "The Reckoner gives comfort. You have to understand what a devastating loss it was for Congaree and Gwyntog when its last Oracle died. Until that time, people believed that someone with ultimate knowledge watched over them. When Aven, the last Oracle, died, a Regent was appointed in his stead—the Reckoner. There has been a Reckoner in each province for generations now. But unlike the Oracles, he has no unusual abilities."

"I thought you didn't believe that nonsense about Oracles," said Anders.

"I believe the Oracles were real," said Pask. "No serious historian would dispute their existence."

"You really believe they were psychic?"

"Not psychic," said Pask. "Omniscient."

"And they had congress with dragons?" said Anders.

"In a manner of speaking," said Pask. "The History texts were not meant to be taken literally. The dragons did exist. They were distant cousins of the estuarine crocodile, so Shorey tells me. The seat of the Oracle's power lay in his relationship with the dragons. I've heard Shorey explain it in Biological terms. He thinks that the dragons carried a fatal plague which they passed to the Oracles. The Oracles were genetically immune and hence the Oracular post was passed down through a single family line; it didn't make them sick, but it killed anyone they touched. And of course, it gave them the power of prophecy."

"You believe that?"

"Yes," said Pask. "And it's because of that that I don't believe there is a God."

"I don't follow."

"Consider: If the Oracle were omniscient, he would have known if there were a God. If there is no God, then why did no Oracle ever say so? If there is one, why did they keep silent about it?"

"What would be the point?" said Anders. "People who believe in God aren't going to stop believing no matter what they're told. People who don't believe won't suddenly become believers because they've been told He exists by some know-it-all."

"What about the people who don't know what to believe, the ones who *need* a sign? The ones who wait for faith to claim them? Why didn't the Oracles help them?"

"Don't look at me," said Anders. "I'd rather not know."

Pask lit a cigarette, and they sat for a time in silence as the smoke collected in the stuffy room. "Was that why you came to see me, to talk about Truth and Knowledge?"

"I'm sorry," said Anders. "I don't know why I lost my temper today." But he did know. For a moment, when Bilbury had spoken to him, he had felt an uncontrollable rage at being interrupted from his daydream of the *Verdegris* hands. He felt a whisper of that anger still, talking to Pask.

Talk of the Reckoner brought something else to his mind. "There *was* something I was wondering," said Anders. "The Reckoner wears red gloves. So did the Oracles. Why?"

"Red hands signify omniscience," said Pask.

"Truth or Knowledge?"

"Both," said Pask. "But in the Reckoner's case it's only symbolic. In the Oracle's case, it was literal. The gloves were also a warning to people that his touch could kill. It was how the plague was transmitted."

"What do you know about those old houses out in the woods?"

"The ones past the boathouse? They're the old dormitories from decades ago."

"Have you been inside them?" said Anders, watching him intently.

Shaka Pask flicked the ash from his cigarette and contemplated it. "Were you suggesting a field trip? For historical interest, of course."

"For historical interest, yes," said Anders.

The next morning, quite early, Anders watched as Shaka Pask stood at the door to *Verdegris*. He wore a grubby yellow and gray striped jersey and equally grubby shorts. He was holding a heavy pry bar.

"All right?" he said to Anders. He flicked the stub of his cigarette into the bushes.

"All right," said Anders.

The door was shut and locked this time, but Shaka Pask produced a key on a ring large enough for a bull's nose. "From the dean's own hand," he said. "If we find anything useful, we're to let him know. I wonder how he defines 'useful.'"

Pask unlocked the door and went inside. He stood in the foyer, pry bar swinging like a pendulum. Anders watched him, tense, expecting him to go up the stairs, but instead he stalked off into the dimness of one of the main floor rooms. He was barely out of sight before Anders bolted up the stairs. He could not get up them fast enough. He neither stopped nor slowed until he reached the last curve of the staircase under the skylight. There, he caught his breath.

The hands were still in their glassed-in column. The red paint on the bones, if that was what it was, looked brighter than he remembered, gleaming like lacquer. A covetous yearning stirred in him. But the moment he put his palms to the glass, he heard Pask shouting below.

Pask didn't matter. Anders pressed his palms against the glass, felt for seams, seeking a way to open the column. But the glass was smooth, flawless, and would not yield. Anders tensed, applied more force, and felt the want for those skeletal hands deepening. He looked around him and saw, for one moment, a pry bar lying on the step below him. He reached for it, and his fingers closed around nothing. The bar was gone.

A clatter of footsteps echoed in the stairwell. "Anders!" Anders felt himself shoved, and he stumbled.

Anders looked up to see Pask below him on the stairs, holding the pry bar in his hand. "What?!"

"I've found something," Pask panted. "Come on." He hooked the pry bar around Anders' shoulder and tugged at him as he started back down the stairs.

Anders didn't move.

Pask turned around, tugged again. "Come on."

"Why?"

"I need your help to open this crate, that's why. What's the matter with you?"

"What's the matter with *you*?"

He watched Pask carefully, but Pask's eyes met his, never once strayed to the hands in their display case. *Clever*, thought Anders. *He knows they're there, but he's pretending he hasn't seen.*

"Come on, Anders." Pask turned and trotted down the stairs, looking back to make sure that Anders followed him. Reluctantly, Anders did.

Pask showed him to the room he'd explored on his first visit to the house. Anders stood in the doorway and watched as Pask applied the pry bar to the packing crate nearest the window.

Anders winced as the wood splintered. Pask gripped the broken edge of a board with his hand and ripped it free, widening the hole. The floor was already strewn with splintered debris. Pask worked at the crate like a lion disemboweling a wildebeest.

"There's something inside," said Pask. "But it's too heavy for me to get out. I'll make the gap wider, and you can help me drag it out."

Anders stole a glance toward the stairs. The wood popped explosively, and a cloud of dust spurted out as Pask pried another slat free. Pask flung the pry bar across the floor. "We should be able to get at it now. Wake up, Anders."

Anders stared at the pry bar on the floor. Pask gripped his shoulder and brought him down to his knees next to the crate. Pask guided his hands inside the gap he'd made in the crate to something with the texture of sack cloth. Together, they pulled it towards them until Pask could get his hands further in.

Pask struggled with it briefly, then froze. "Something's loose inside," he whispered.

Anders felt it too, fragile yet hard in his hands. Pask fumbled for a moment, and then together they withdrew the object from the crate. They held it cupped in their hands, round, shaggy with tattered paper. Pask took it from Anders, tore it away, a handful at a time and the paper thickened and darkened and became soft muslin, black silk. Each of these layers Pask peeled away and let drop onto the floor until he held in his hands what looked like a small, dark bowl. He brought it to one of the windows.

Anders heard a rustling in the far corner of the room. He peered into the dimness looking for rats, but all he saw was the pry bar Pask had cast aside, lying in shadow against the wall.

"And there it is," said Pask, and Anders turned to see him holding an object up to the light.

For a moment, Anders was struck by the silhouette that Pask cut, holding it over his head like a trophy. A primal image of triumph.

The sunlight shone around it, broke through it and Anders realized what it was at last. Not a bowl, but a cup. A glass cup. He went cold.

Pask lowered his arms and knelt on the floor, and in that moment, he became again the man Anders knew, though he seemed now quieter, more sober. Pask set the cup on the floor tenderly.

Anders bolted for the stairs, tore up them three at a time until, panting, he reached the top. The hands… the hands were still there. But now, they held nothing.

That evening, Anders let himself into the school library and consulted a textbook on Anatomy. When he was finished, on an impulse, he went through some old historical records from the school's past and located some handwritten index cards referring to the old dormitories. Pask had let slip that eighty years previously, someone had inventoried the contents of the various dormitories. Of the hands, he could find no written record, but he came across something interesting about the object which Anders believed to have been held in those skeletal hands:

Catalogue #1-09745 A. In Storage: one small vessel, volcanic glass, green, Congaree. Use unknown, most likely dating from the mid-to-late Oracular Aven Dynasty. This piece was found in a shipment from a private estate where it was stored during the war. Box labeled 'Black Tor', donated by the late Arthur Dean in 1923.

Poring over the rest of the catalogue, Anders was no wiser as to the origin of the hands. Had they been holding the cup before Pask had come up the stairs behind him? He could not remember now, he had been so intent on the hands themselves. Could someone have moved the cup, put it downstairs in the crate? And if so, why?

Something was making him very uneasy. It wasn't until he had returned to his room and found the history text lying open where he had left it that he remembered now why he'd recognized the name 'Black Tor'.

He consulted the History text. Among its many charms, it had no index. After an hour, he found the reference. It was from the lesson he'd been preparing on the day he had found the hands:

...and the Oracle went into the Tower at Black Tor and had congress with the dragon therein and emerged with the gift of prophecy...

So, Black Tor was where the dragon lived. Anders flipped through the book absently and the name 'Aven' caught his eye. He remembered it from the catalogue card. According to the text, Aven was the last Oracle. As near as Anders could make out—the wording was not at all clear—he had ended his life by cutting his wrists at the age of 22. There was some speculation that the mantle of Truth had become too heavy for him to bear. Anders shuddered, read on.

Black Tor had been sealed. The place had become a kind of Mecca. But people feared it too. The memory of the plague the Oracle had carried remained, and no one dared enter it.

That cup, thought Anders, came from Black Tor.

As Anders closed the book, a triangle of torn paper floated free. He retrieved it. It had been torn from one of the pages in the text; across the back of it he recognized the typeface. Scrawled on the other side of the paper were the words: *Pask wants you dead. Don't go back to Verdegris....*

The note was in Anders' handwriting.

Anders was standing on the staircase in Verdegris.

"Morning, Sir," the boys chorused.

"Morning," said Anders.

Most of the boys trooped past him, but a few lagged behind on the staircase where Anders stood.

"What are they?" said Anders, pointing to the skeletal hands in their case.

"Those belong to Aven, the school's founder, Sir," said Bilbury. "Tradition, Sir. All the boys who graduate leave their hands to the school when they die. They've got loads of them, Sir, up in the attic." He spoke with some degree of authority.

"Liar!" said another boy. "Those are the devil's hands. Everyone who's ever touched them went mad, Sir. That's why they've sealed them up in there."

Anders gave the hands a longing look. Through the glass the red was even more intense, so intense the bones appeared to be throbbing.

Anders blinked, opened his eyes wide. He was lying in bed in his lodgings with the dawn light shining between the curtains he had forgotten to pull closed. He still felt the throbbing, but it was now inside his chest.

Later that day, Anders noticed that one of his boys was absent from the class. He mentally consulted his class list: Bilbury.

Thinking about it, he couldn't remember seeing the boy in class the day before either. The subdued air of the boys was subsumed by an air of tension.

"Where's Bilbury?" Anders demanded.

"Dead, Sir," said one of the boys.

"Not yet, Sir," said one of the others.

"He's in the infirmary, Sir."

Anders met Pask halfway across the football pitch.

"Bilbury," said Anders.

"I don't think for much longer," said Pask.

"You knew?"

"You didn't."

"What's going on, Pask?"

"I caught him inside *Verdegris* the other day," said Pask, lighting a cigarette without breaking stride.

"What…? What was he doing there?"

"He claimed he went there on a dare. He was on the stairs when I caught him. I wasn't going to inform the dean, but the next thing I heard, he was deathly ill. I'm just going to see if he's faking to avoid a suspension or whether it's genuine." Anders noticed that Pask didn't quite meet his eyes.

"Pask," said Anders. "Did he have anything with him when you caught him?"

Pask blew a single ring of smoke and shook his head. "No worries," he said. "It's not there any more."

"What's not there any more?"

"What we found. It's in a safe place."

Which put Anders' mind in turmoil. He had felt edgy enough knowing that Pask knew about the hands. But Bilbury. Bilbury must have seen them. Now everyone would find out about them. Too much was at stake. Too many people knew.

That evening in the dining hall for example, he overheard a conversation.

"But what was he doing in *Verdegris* anyway? There's nothing in there," said one of the lecturers.

"Not completely correct," said Shorey. "During the war, a number of national treasures were parceled up and shipped along the coast after Congaree was bombed. They wound up in various country estates. Some of them came here. The dormitories weren't being used so the dean at the time turned them into repositories. Of course, all of it was supposed to have been reclaimed after the war, but it never happened."

"Well, whatever he was doing there, it must be kept quiet," said the dean. "I don't want any of this repeated, especially now. Especially since it's got nothing to do with what's happened. Excuse me." The dean stood up and left. He looked shaken, pale.

"What's with him?" said Anders, forcing a casual tone.

"Hadn't you heard?" said Shorey. "Bilbury died this evening."

Anders planned his return to *Verdegris* meticulously. He chose the day of Bilbury's memorial service when everyone would be in the chapel.

The clouds lay heavy and low with unwept rain. In the distance, towards the sea, the sky had gone a deep, navy blue. The impending storm had silenced the birds in the wood. Anders winced at the sound of his shoes crushing the grass, and sticking to the gravel path.

Inside *Verdegris*, echoes filled the stairwell, the sound of inhalation and exhalation, as though the place breathed with him. Upstairs where the hands waited for him, the sunlight no longer danced perfect rainbows in the air. The light filtered through the window in violets and blues, the colors of water and ice.

Anders had cut a piece of wooden doweling, using his own hand as a model to estimate the proper length. He had bored a hole through the doweling lengthwise, painted it red using acrylics borrowed from the Arts teacher, then threaded a wire through the hole. He hadn't been sure about the gauge and had had to experiment with a few until he found a thickness he thought strong enough. A tube of model glue waited in his shirt pocket.

The glass cabinet had a cunningly disguised sliding panel. He found it easily now, as though it had been waiting until he was worthy, to reveal itself. It slid back obligingly, and he was greeted with a smell like a cold roast. His hands were trembling.

He paused and listened for the sound of footsteps on the stairs, the creak of a door opening. Instead, the skeletal hands themselves trembled, vibrating ever so slightly, as though in recognition of what he was about to do. As though they were still alive. They trembled more violently, and with their movement came the sound of thunder growing in the distance. It went on for some time. He waited until the hands went still, then he put on a pair of gardening gloves and pulled a pair of wire cutters from his back pocket. After poring over an Anatomy book, he had elected to take the first metacarpal bone, a bone inside the hand itself, not in the finger. It was the most aesthetic bone in the hand. He wanted it, and he wanted it intact.

Anders grasped it with his thumb and index finger. As soon as he touched it, he felt heat through the fingertips of his glove as though the bone had just come out of an oven. He let go, felt a surge of excitement and need. He grasped the bone again, more firmly, decisively, and set the cutters against the wire where it joined the metacarpal to the wrist. He squeezed the cutters, but the wire was strong. He clenched his hand, grimacing, gripped the cutters with both fists, squeezing until his hands were searing hot and threaded with pain. And then the jaws of the cutters closed, like a gun detonating, and the bones dropped to the shelf.

Anders looked with a degree of dread at the broken hands. He grabbed the bones he had cut free, the metacarpal with the three bones of the finger all attached to it. He used the wire cutters to snip them from the coveted metacarpal, and then thrust it quickly into his pocket. The air smelt of sun-baked flesh and burnt bone, the aftertaste of stressed metal. Anders set the doweling and its wire against the broken end of the wire which protruded from the wrist like a petrified vein. He squeezed a drop of contact cement in place and held the doweling, counting, while the seconds oozed past. He felt compelled to hurry, was terrified of being sloppy. He released the doweling and surveyed his work. The glue held, but the doweling sat at the wrong angle. There was no time to fix it. Anders glued the finger bones—phalanges, the Anatomy text had called them—to the free end of the doweling. He could barely hold them steady as the glue set.

He closed the glass cabinet. A glance told him enough; he'd not done the job well. Anyone looking would surely be able to see that the hand had been tampered with.

He descended the stairs with his prize clutched in his fist. He opened the door to the bloom of a storm. The trees behind *Verdegris* were tossing in the wind. He couldn't see them, but he heard them as they struggled frantically.

He shut the door and ran along the path into the wood. It was not only guilt that drove him; in the lull of the wind, he'd heard footsteps behind him. He ran faster through the dimness in the trees. They shook their heavy branches at him, leaves coming free.

He broke from the trees into a clearing. A lake stood before him. On the slope leading down to the shore was an old stone hut too small to be a house. The first drops of rain slashed his cheek, his cuffs. It began slicing down. He looked at his rain-sodden cuffs. They were gray, like smoke; this wasn't ordinary rain. The clouds were bleeding ash. Anders ran for the hut. The door was off its hinges, as though someone had been at it before. Anders kicked it viciously, shoved his way inside and then ground the door back into place behind him. Rain roared on the roof.

Anders stayed with his back pressed against the wood. Whoever was following him might try to get in. He breathed choking breaths. The rain on the roof sounded like a choir singing nonsense. One hand went to his pocket and found the bone, held it tight. *Make a wish, Anders.*

Two days later, Anders went to see Pask.

"Is it true?" said Anders.

"That I've been sacked? Yes. Come inside."

Anders sat on the Pask's frumpy settee and slipped his hand into his pocket. He'd taken to keeping the metacarpal there. It fit perfectly in his grasp, like it belonged there, and he felt anxiety building whenever he wasn't touching it.

Pask nudged a bowl of striped peppermints towards Anders. "Sweet?"

Anders grimaced. "Thanks, no."

"Tea, then?" said Pask.

"Yes, all right," said Anders.

Pask returned not a minute later holding two cups. He set one on the coffee table.

"That was quick," said Anders.

"I knew you were coming," said Pask. Pask lifted his own cup, a heavy hemispherical thing, and looked at Anders. "To complicity."

Anders sipped his tea. His own rose-patterned cup looked far more civilized than what Pask was using.

"'Let there be no strife between me and thee—'" said Pask.

Through the light from the window, he saw that Pask's cup, though primitive and bowl-shaped, was also polished and beautiful.

"Is that the… thing you found in *Verdegris*?"

"Well done," said Pask.

"Pask, what happened? Why did the dean sack you?"

"I think the dean needed a scapegoat for Bilbury's death. I was ready to hand."

"That's ludicrous!"

"Have you ever read the bible, Anders?"

"I try to avoid anything dealing with religion in case you hadn't noticed. Why?"

"You know about the Holy Grail?"

"I've heard of it. What are you getting at?"

Pask shrugged and put his cup down on the table. "Some people," said Pask, "like to preach absolute Truth without actually understanding what it means. What the Oracles had wasn't an ability to alter time. They could simply look down the paths at the end of certain choices and see what would come about as a result of those choices. Ordinary men make choices blindly. The Oracle saw the consequences of every choice, because for him, to consider them was to live through them, every one. Imagine being the Oracle. Imagine having access to important information that other people wanted, *needed*. Granting guidance to great leaders, great people, having a hand in making the greatest decisions of your day, shaping the times. Knowing the Truth and sharing it with everyone. Do you know how Congaree's last Oracle met his end, Anders?"

"Look Pask, you've lost your job. What are you going to do?"

"Nothing," said Pask. "The dean won't follow through. They're too short-staffed to let me go before the end of term. You didn't answer *my* question though, Anders."

"About what?"

"The Oracle. Why were you so keen to leave England and come here to teach?"

Anders felt his body tighten. "Pardon me?"

"Sacrifice is all very noble, but self-sacrifice is pointless." Pask smiled at him, like a co-conspirator; his expression evoked an intimacy which Anders found offensive.

"Why don't you go fuck yourself," said Anders.

"What happened to all your noble talk of Truth?" said Pask.

"I never lied."

"Avoiding the Truth is no better. You should embrace it." There was something intent and sinister in the way Pask was looking at him.

"Stay out of my business," said Anders, standing, "and stay away from me. Don't tell me how to deal with my life." Anders shoved the door shut behind him.

Embrace the Truth. He could imagine what that would have done to his family, facing it or avoiding it the way he'd contemplated. And Pask… He shuddered, felt sick. That affinity he'd felt between them was tainted now.

Anders woke with a start. The covers were heaped on the floor, the curtains wide, and the wind was billowing great gusts against the windows hard enough to make the glass creak. On his desk, the text of Gwyntog and the Marches lay open. Anders blinked.

He played over his memories of Pask and found himself lost. Something had passed between them that evening, something unsettling, but he couldn't fully comprehend what it was.

He became aware of a burning sensation in his right hand. Against the whiteness of the sheets, it looked darker than it ought to be. He turned it over, peered at his palm; something wasn't quite right. Without touching his skin, he could feel his pulse throbbing in his wrist, could *see* it. His fingertips felt like they ought to be throwing sparks, like the nerves were awakening after a long sleep.

He looked at it under his desk lamp and confirmed that it was dark red. He scrubbed his hand with a nailbrush and soap, but the water ran clear from it. His frantic scrubbing had intensified the pain. He filled his sink with ice water and held his hand there. The pain worsened alarmingly, and he had to withdraw it.

He sat at his desk with his hand swaddled in a coldwater-soaked towel. In his other hand, he held his stolen bone. His fingertips felt as though pins had been driven through them under the fingernails.

The infirmary consisted of four cots in an overly large and airless room. Pask lay, eyes open, on the only occupied cot. Anders didn't recognize him at first out of his yellow and gray jersey and with his head wrapped in white. Coming closer, Anders discerned more subtle changes in his appearance. A slow kind of shock seized him. Pask's face was deeply and darkly flushed, his features distorted as though from a heavy blow. The tips of his fingers, where they lay on the sheet beside him were deep blue-red. Anders fancied he could feel the heat of the blood pooling under Pask's skin.

"Come to finish the job?" said Pask.

Anders felt a weight in his hand, looked down and saw that he was holding a pry bar, and it was dripping.

"You want to interfere in my life—"

"Mister Anders," said the matron. She seemed upset to see him there.

Anders turned quickly. "I want to speak to the doctor."

"We have no doctor here," said the matron. "There's a local doctor at Bay of Birds. He comes to us once a month."

"What about him?" said Anders, gesturing to the bed.

"Mister Anders. That patient has been dead for half an hour."

And then Anders saw on the bed, where he had before seen Pask, now lay the body of Bilbury.

He got himself out of there somehow. Leaning back against the door, he felt in his pocket for the comforting presence of the bone. It wasn't there, though he clearly remembered putting it there. He needed it. He had not realized how much he needed its contact until he had lost it. Frantically he searched his other pockets, but could not find it.

A nders crossed the football pitch in a state of disarray. He passed a group of boys practicing on the field. He couldn't risk them noticing him. His air of relaxed haste was a facade, one that could not be maintained under close scrutiny.

Reaching *Verdegris* at last, he shouldered open the door. He went inside without stopping to shut it. It was only a hundred steps to the fifth floor, but when he reached the second landing, he felt a biting cramp stab deep in his gut. He pulled himself up by the stair railing, his hand tingling like starlight and ground glass.

Reaching the final twist of the stairs, he stopped, made an inarticulate cry of dismay. The display case was empty. The hands, gone. *Pask*, he thought then. *Pask took them.*

But when he peered closely at the case, he realized that it wasn't empty at all. Instead, in the dim light, the case seemed full of mottled shadow; it looked as though a tomato had burst inside it. The tingling in his hand intensified.

He looked at his hand. The sleeve of his shirt, which he'd pulled down over his hand, was dripping blood. He watched the drops strike the stair by his foot. Cautiously, like a child winding a jack-in-the-box, he pulled back the cuff. A warning, awakening shrill of pain spidered his arm as he twitched it free. He was looking at the *Verdegris* hands. The *Verdegris* hands were *his* hands, red, stripped, one of them missing a bone that had been clipped free.

"Oh…" he said. The stair rail pressed cold against him. He slid down it like it was greased until he bumped the foot of the landing. He began to hyper-ventilate. As he stared at the floor, he heard footsteps, saw a pair of cleated shoes step into his line of sight. They were covered in mud. Then a pair of hairy knees descended and Pask was kneeling in front of him.

Pask plucked at Anders' sleeve, looked appraisingly at it. "Shook hands with Aven, did you?" He laughed without smiling. "Just let things be. Don't think, don't analyze, don't ask questions. Before you know it, you'll have more answers than you'll know what to do with."

"I just…"

"Don't bother explaining yourself." Pask's voice was now close, loud and intimate in his ear. "Take it as read that I know already."

The air went thick and hot. Anders' vision grayed and tingled. He tried, feebly to push Pask away.

Anders was lying down in a place he didn't know. It was dark except for the dying fluorescent bulb above him that threw flashes like heat lightning over the sheets. Someone had tucked them in tight around him. He could hear the rhythmic hum of some kind machinery and the listless breath of a ceiling fan, and echoes. He was in a room, a large one. When he saw the bars along the side of the bed and felt the plastic bracelet on his wrist, and saw the accordion pleats of the nylon curtains swaying silently beside his bed, he realized where he must be. He could move only his eyes, and even that was difficult. He was in no pain, but there was a curious deadness about his body, a heavy lethargy. His hands, where they lay on the sheet, were intact, but deep red, swollen with blood.

And then the curtain rattled back and a man in yellow and gray entered his space. The man leaned over the bed, grasped the railing with a red-gloved hand, and when he saw that Anders' eyes were open, he spoke a word that Anders did not understand. He repeated it, louder. "Anders?"

It seemed not to matter. Anders was unable to speak, and it was too much effort to keep his eyes open, so he let them close. At some point, from the darkness he was sinking into, Anders heard a voice. "You're in hospital in Bay of Birds."

Anders concentrated on breathing; it seemed most important, but he could still hear the man's voice, coming between him and a far-off image of green hills.

Instinct told him that something inside had gone wrong and that the implications were serious, probably mortal.

"I was telling you that the gift we share is too big to be confined to this little stretch of coast."

Anders heard him, but it was like listening to someone recite a lesson he had long since memorized. He knew very well what Pask was going to say, knew what Pask knew. That in some age long past, an Oracle named Aven had taken his own life. Aven had known what was going to happen after he died. So he bled out his wisdom into a vessel. A cup of enlightenment. He left it in Black Tor. He knew that someone worthy would discover it. He also knew that someone unworthy might find it first. But that could not be helped.

"People need to know," said Pask. "People must be told."

But he was telling Anders nothing new. Pask saw all that could be done with their knowledge—adopted children reunited with their birth parents. Anders saw how Pask saw that sharing this knowledge was a thing that had to be done, how spreading the Truth was a duty he was bound to perform. And Anders saw only the pain and disillusionment that would cause. Some things in the world were better left unsaid.

"But it didn't happen that way," said Anders, sitting forward on Pask's settee.

"Have you ever been physically sick after you've eaten something?" said Pask. "Even something you used to like?"

"Peppermint-flavored sweets said Anders. "Your point?"

"How do you feel when you try to remember the last time you ate one?"

"Sick," said Anders. "Obviously."

"But the last time you ate one was before you became sick, before you made the association between that flavor and feeling sick. At the time you had it, you probably enjoyed it."

"Your point?" said Anders.

"Knowledge you acquire in the present influences your perceptions of the past. We revise our memories to reflect what we now know. The past, as we perceive it, is constantly changing."

"If I can't trust my memories—"

"We can't change the past; it only feels that way. We can only tell what might be, for any given choice."

"**C**ome to finish the job?" said Pask.

"Yes," said Anders, and he swung the pry bar.

Choke Point

First published in *Fantasy Magazine*, December 2009.

Steve was just north of Chaffeys Lock driving back from Rachel's house in Ottawa when he saw the snake on the road. If he'd been with Rachel he wouldn't have stopped. Rachel wouldn't have noticed it, but if he had pointed it out to her, she would have shut her eyes and ordered him to drive on. But Rachel wasn't with him, so he pulled the truck onto the soft shoulder and got out.

Black rat snakes liked to bask on the road and soak up the warmth there. This one, over a meter and a half in length, lay width-wise across the road. Likely, the driver who had hit it had mistaken it for a line of tar sealing a crack in the asphalt, a narrow band of darkness on the hot blacktop, an insignificant bump under the tires. Or maybe the driver had done it deliberately.

Steve listened for traffic. In the marsh across the road, a red-winged blackbird called out *conga-ree*, flashing its scarlet epaulettes. Otherwise this stretch of road was quiet. Steve crouched down next to the snake. Its body had been crushed about five centimeters behind its head. Its skin had split open, a gaping slit that was bright red inside like the cut pomegranates Rachel ate for breakfast. The asphalt was darkened and tacky under his shoes where the snake had bled. Greenbottle flies studded its body like living jewels.

Steve retrieved his work gloves and a plastic bucket from the back of his truck. Carefully, he pulled the snake from the road. It stuck where it had been run over, and he had to lift it delicately to keep it intact. He lowered it reverently into the bucket, coiling the body inside. Once it was all in, he laid a burlap sack over the top to keep the flies off and replaced the bucket on the bed of the truck. Then he headed for home. Home, but not for much longer.

As he drove he brushed the back of the passenger seat where Jed usually rode, felt the bristling carpet of black and white hairs that had resisted multiple vacuumings. He looked out the passenger side window, through the smudges of Jed's nose-prints on the glass. He felt the absence like a missing tooth. *Get used to it*, he told himself.

He shouldn't have picked up that snake; he didn't have time to deal with it properly. He had other things to do. Packing, for instance.

It would have been a waste, though, to have left it there. A pointless, unnatural death. This way, after he'd cleaned the skeleton, it could go to a museum, a university, or to a naturalist, like Steve, who would use it to educate people about local fauna.

Steve drove up the long laneway to his house. He saw his house with new eyes each time he came back from a visit to Rachel's. He didn't used to think about it; it was just home. After he'd brought Rachel here and seen her reaction, the comments she'd visibly refrained from making, he now saw it as small and shabby.

Steve lifted the bucket from the back of the truck. Jed stood at the fence, white tail a blur of motion, his nose with its pale patch of pink, pressed into the chain link. Jed greeted Steve at the gate, sniffing the bucket, then him. Jed followed Steve out to the workshop in the shed at the back of the yard.

Steve had to make a decision: how best to deal with the snake. He wanted to clean the skeleton in the most efficient way. Carrion beetles would do the job for him, but that could take weeks, and he'd sold his stock of carrion beetles the week before. Alternately, the carcass could be put into a plastic bag filled with water, tied closed and left for a few months. As long as you made sure you when you opened the bag, you were in a well ventilated area.

The third method was to boil the carcass. It was messy and labor-intensive, but it was also quick. As Steve was moving out in two days, this was the only option.

As he went to the house, he saw Jed run over to his doghouse and wolf the kibble in his bowl. Steve watched him grimly; he'd paid the neighbor to put out food for Jed in the morning and evening while he was in Ottawa, but obviously, it didn't matter; Jed refused to eat when Steve wasn't home.

In the house, Steve dug through boxes of his camping gear until he found his hunting knife and a couple of old, banged-up pots. Rachel wouldn't let anything like those into her kitchen with her ornamental copper pots and marble counter tops.

He filled the pots with water and set them on the stove. He did his best to cut away as much of the skin and muscle from the skeleton as he could; the more work he did by hand, the less work the boiling water would have to do.

He cut the carcass where it had been flattened and divided the smooth black body between the two pots of water, putting the head aside. Once he'd got the water boiling, he put lids on the pots. Then he emptied the spare bedroom and the kitchen cupboards, packing his remaining things into boxes. He kept an eye on the clock. Boil the carcass too long and all the little bones would come apart, and reassembling them would be an exercise in migraine generation.

At last, he returned to the stove, turned the heat off under the pots, then he called Jed out to the truck.

He drove down to the abandoned CN line. The tracks had been taken up years ago leaving gravel and a road that was decompressing from underneath. He drove carefully, straddling the big sinkhole that had been forming for the past three months. He stopped where the road opened up to either side and below where he had a view of the water. He opened the truck door, and Jed piled out.

It was three PM, the sky a fading blue. For some reason, it was always colder here than anywhere else along the road, no matter what time of year it was. He looked out over the water.

Some people were afraid of the enormity of the place when they came out here at night, but Steve felt that it was a privilege to be a part of this. He didn't have much, but he'd wanted to give this to Rachel, to her children: take them up here to see it. But they hadn't wanted it.

"It's not *us*," Rachel had said, with the implication that he was included in the 'us.' That was a strange feeling.

He'd been taking Jed out here nearly every day for eight years. Once, they'd seen a coyote standing boldly broadside-on to them on the road not twenty meters away. Jed had gone crazy, barking, and Steve had barely caught him in time, stopping him from lunging forward. A coyote would sometimes lure a dog out to the rest of the pack so that they could kill it.

In all the years he'd had Jed that had been the closest he'd come to losing him. Steve had bought him from a kid selling puppies out of a cardboard box at the livestock market. Four of them when Steve had walked by on his way in, a tumble of black and white; one left on the way out—the one no one else had wanted. Small enough to fit in the pocket of his bush jacket.

Steve walked down the abandoned road. He could hear the ringing call of a toad, then another. No more walks like this after tonight. No more breathing air that was so clean you drank it like cold water.

"You can't keep living like this forever, Steve," one of his married friends had said. "Alone in the middle of nowhere. You need a family."

Steve liked children. He brought his specimens to elementary schools sometimes, taught them about natural history. Once they got over their initial squeamishness, most of them took to it. Steve liked Rachel's daughters well enough too, though neither of them had taken to what he did; Rachel hadn't really given them a chance.

He was moving to a real house in Ottawa. He'd never lived in a city before, but this was what was expected of him, that eventually he would have to grow up and accept responsibility. He was thirty-five; his friends had drifted off, paired off, and gradually, very gradually, he'd gone from seeing them regularly to barely seeing them at all, and the only one he spoke to some days was Jed.

He called Jed from wherever he was—he was in the habit of darting into the undergrowth after rabbits; last week he'd found a porcupine in amidst the sumac along the side of the road. Jed came racing back, toenails scattering the gravel.

Steve got back into the truck, shut the door. He looked back over the valley. He took a good, long time doing it, because he knew it would be the last time; he couldn't come here again, not without Jed.

"Love is about sacrifice," Rachel had said. "Love means giving things up for the one you care about."

Steve looked at the keys dangling from the steering column. He felt suddenly like there was a vice grip on his ribs, pain, somewhere so deep he couldn't point to it. He couldn't breathe.

The feeling passed. He turned the key. When he returned to the house, the smell of boiled snake greeted him. In the pots, loose, white trails of flesh jostled and floated like gauze. He ran cold water over them, fished a chunk out with a pair of tongs. He put it on a plate and took it out to the workshop behind the house. Jed followed at his heels.

The shovel stood against the side of the shed, edged with dirt from the grave he'd dug the day before.

Setting the plate on the workbench, he realized that he had made a mistake. It would take hours just to clean the bones. Never mind sorting the 400-odd vertebrae in the correct order. He had other things he had to do tonight, before the light faded. Yet he'd gone too far to just throw it all out.

The pieces of flesh were slippery and Steve had to be careful with his knife. Jed watched him intently, his chin resting on Steve's leg.

Bone were little miracles. Complete, perfect, formed in the darkness under their blankets of skin and muscle, in the womb or the egg. No one ever saw them, until they were revealed like this.

Rachel had been logical. She had custody of the girls, and she was allergic to dogs. Jed was bonded to Steve, wouldn't even eat when Steve wasn't there. It would be a subtle kind of cruelty to give him away, one that Steve could never inflict on Jed.

Steve disarticulated the ribs from the snake's backbone. Freeing each one, he dried it with a dishtowel and laid it on his work table to dry. The body of each rib was smooth, perfectly curved. Except when he came to the part of the snake where it had been flattened under the car tire; these ribs were in fragments. Steve set the piece of snake down.

Better that he not suffer at all.

He turned on his second desk lamp with the magnifier. The rib he'd pulled loose with his forceps had fractured in three pieces. It would be unfair to put broken pieces into the bone box with the rest of the skeleton; Steve ought to repair it first. He rummaged in one of the boxes for some contact cement. He didn't have time for this; the light was fading, and he needed good light to be sure of his aim.

He glanced through the window. The darkness seethed between the trees in the back forty where he'd take Jed out hunting with him. He recalled how in Ottawa Rachel always pulled the curtains closed at the first hint of darkness so that the neighbors couldn't look in. There was nothing but a wooded hill behind his workshop, multi-colored in the autumn and silver with snow in the winter. The kind of view that deserved to be painted. He'd dug the grave out there, in amongst the silver birch.

It was going to be dark soon; better to do it while the light was good.

Steve tapped his forceps on the work table. Fix the broken rib, then do it. He dabbed a bead of contact cement onto the fractured edge of the rib.

Then he picked up the second piece and fit it to the broken edge of the other piece. Something caught his eye. He looked at it through the magnifier on the light. An undulating groove ran along the bone—something that had no right to be there. The fracture truncated it. The third and final rib fragment lay on the plate. Using his forceps he held that one in place while it set. The groove now stretched unbroken along the bone, like an inscription: *Do not forsake me.*

Steve put the rib back onto the plate and switched off the desk lamp. His gun was in the locked cabinet back in the house; he'd refrained from packing it, knowing he would need it one more time before he left here.

Steve got up, and Jed followed him out of the workshop.

Steve packed the last of the boxes into the back of his pickup. He'd sold the house, was due out today; contracts signed, no turning back. He got into the truck, started it up, and drove away from the house, away from Ottawa, away from Rachel and her own responsibilities.

Because love means giving things up for the one you care about.

He looked over at Jed, and Jed's tail thumped on the seat.

The Bone Fisher's Apprentice

First published in *Writers of the Future, Volume XXII.*
Honorable Mention, *Year's Best Fantasy & Horror*, 2007.

The Bone Fisher could slip his hand into water without throwing a ripple. It was an art his apprentice was still mastering.

Sitting down to dinner, sharing the dead seagull they had found on the beach, the apprentice watched him spoon the meat from the gull's body. He did it neatly, without cutting and without touching its feathers. He didn't wait for it to cool before he ate it. Dealing with being burned was another art the apprentice was learning.

"Tell me about people," said the apprentice.

"There are three kinds of people," he told her. "The first kind—the oldest kind—want to be rescued." Another spoonful of steaming gull muscle disappeared into his frog-like mouth. "The second kind want to do the rescuing." He went on chewing.

"And the third kind?" she prompted him.

"The third kind want to be left the hell alone. And God help you if you bother one of them."

"Which kind am I?" she asked. She knew very well which kind she was, but whenever she asked, he would tell her the story of how he found her....

It was the custom in that day and age to bring unwanted babies—those born out of wedlock, the unwanted, the misshapen—to the beach and leave them there for the tide to take. The Bone Fisher took no notice of them. As living, innocent beings with no memories, they were of no use to him. One particular gray morning, however, when he went out with his bucket looking for lures, he stumbled across a bassinet lodged in a rock outcropping on the edge of a tidal pool. It was apparent why the child had been left there; it had a misshapen head, and the hand that grasped the edge of the bassinet had only three fingers. The child was still alive, though not crying, only blinking its clear eyes. It had been tied securely into the bassinet with two gray ribbons crossed and knotted below its chin. The bassinet itself had been unstably set on the edge of the tidal pool which the Fisher himself knew to be waist-deep. The pool never emptied completely even at the perigean tide in the hottest and driest of years.

As the Fisher watched, the child moved and the bassinet tipped, spilling the child into the depths. It sank immediately. The child's mother had obviously taken care to weight the bassinet, leaving nothing to chance.

The Fisher watched slow bubbles breach the surface, tendrils of slipgrass stirring in the child's wake until they went still. He watched for a time before turning away and going back across the sands to the harbor. A few steps he took, then he stopped. Then a few more. Then stopped. One step. He watched the bucket swinging from his hand. He dropped it, and the swag spilled out across the sand. And then he turned and walked back to the tidal pool, stepped into the water, warm as soup, and reached into its depths until he felt the carapace of the bassinet with a great softness of baby inside it. He pulled it up. Then he took the child home.

The Fisher knew nothing of children or of how to look after them, so he fed her body on beach carrion and her mind on the dreams of the elderly to give her wisdom, cynicism, the strength to resist hope. Hope was valueless and potentially dangerous, innocence more so.

He also tried to instill in her, so much as her nature would allow, a toughness of character. He did this by acquainting her with the world's sharpest edges early on. He discovered that though her body was misshapen, and she quite lame, her eyes were keen and sharp, and very tender to the beautiful things hidden among the sand and stones on the beaches. Before she was very old, he began sending her out to gather lures for his nightly fishing. She learned quite young that the best time to go out was at dawn when the beaches were empty, because sometimes when people saw her, they threw stones at her. She was a reminder of the worst that could happen. She learned to take the Fisher's cloak while he slept and cover herself with it whenever she went out. It was so big on her that when she wrapped it tight around herself, no one could see her at all—oh, they knew who she was, but they behaved more respectfully when they couldn't see her deformities. No one would ever attack her directly, of course; they were all too afraid of her master.

So the years passed, and the apprentice grew into young adulthood via a life of ritual: nights of dreams seeded with stolen thoughts, mornings searching and collecting, evenings of questions over a scavenged or stolen dinner. And always the question, "Tell me about people." But never did the Bone Fisher answer her question: *What kind am I?*

On an early morning in summer when the apprentice was seventeen, she was crossing the pebbled beach with her bucket as the sun rose. The lure bucket was small and ceramic, black enamelled on the outside, white on the inside. She would feel the pull of it in her shoulder joint as she carried it, even empty. The tide was ebbing—the best time for searching, as the stones at the water's edge were still wet. There she would find bits of glass, translucent and smooth or frosted. The Bone Fisher thought the green ones best for his purposes—the ones that most appealed to those drifting in dreams. For many people, green was the color of paradise.

The Fisher sent her out for glass, but she also collected colored pebbles, odd ones, blue ones, green ones, ones with fossils embedded in them, peculiar shells. These were for her. She would put them in the pockets of the Fisher's cloak till there was no more room, and it was time to go home.

On this particular day, she had massed a few handfuls of glass in her bucket and one or two notable pebbles, when she found a golden heart in the sand between the stones. When she picked it up, she saw that the heart was a golden locket attached to a fine chain, like the kind lovers give each other. She dipped it into the sea to wash the sand away. The chain was broken, probably how it had come to be here. She tried to pry it open, but couldn't manage it. Pebbles and glass were the enemies of fingernails, and hers had lost the war long ago. The Bone Fisher occasionally used gold for its powerful mesmerizing properites. She should have put it in the bucket for him. Instead, she slipped it into her pocket with the pebbles.

That night, she lay awake trying to imagine the faces of the lovers in the locket. Who were they? Were they people she had seen before, at a distance on the beach? Were they still in love? Were they dead? A week later when she found herself alone in the old watchtower where she lived with the Fisher, she pried the locket open with a knife from the kitchen. There was nothing inside it but a few grains of sand. She was disappointed. It was like some of the pebbles she found on the beach which looked so beautiful and colorful when wet, only to become dull, gray things when the sea had dried on them.

Not long after she found the locket, she made a discovery of another kind. She had just finished her morning's lure-hunting, and the bucket was nearly full of bright nuggets of glass. They were clean because she'd taken a great deal of care to rinse them in the sea, standing there in her shorts while the water flooded the tops of her rubber boots. She always washed the glass just before coming home. It was the best part of her day, to count the fruits of her labor, but it was also the most stressful. By the time she reached this stage, it was well after dawn, the most likely time she would be discovered.

She had just finished washing the glass and was wobbling, one-footed on the stones, emptying the water out of her rubber boot when she saw a man down by the bitches. The bitches were what the townsfolk called the jagged rock islands off the end of the point that lay just under the water at high tide and would rip the bottom out of a boat if you weren't careful. At low tide, they stood right at the water's edge, bared to the gums. The man was sitting on one of these rocks with his bare feet braced on the opposite one. She couldn't tell at first what he was doing. Wisdom dictated that she leave before she was seen, but he seemed so innocuous sitting there, and she found herself suddenly curious to see what he was doing. She moved closer.

He was playing with something long and dark on the sand. Coming closer, she saw it writhing there, glistening, silver and black. It moved like an eel, but didn't look quite like one. The man pinned it to the sand with his toe, and it curled around his foot and slithered up to encircle his ankle. The man pushed off the rocks and turned to go back up the slope. The eel—or watever it was—looked like a ribbon now, still around his ankle. He caught sight of the apprentice and stopped. The apprentice pulled the cloak tight around herself. The man came towards her. He managed the pebbled slope very well for someone without shoes. The apprentice backed away from him. As she did, the wind caught her hood and blew it back from her face.

She had never seen another person at such close quarters before. He looked perhaps old enough to have small children.

The apprentice pulled her hood up quickly.

"I've seen worse," said the man. He said it like a challenge. "What's your name?"

She knew about the concept of naming; she swam in enough dreams and nightmares to know it. "I don't have a name. I'm the Bone Fisher's apprentice."

"What's in there?" said the man, pointing to her bucket.

"Lures, for the Fisher," she said. "I collect them." She wasn't sure whether this was strictly a secret. No one had ever asked her before.

"Oh," said the man, as though he had solved a puzzle. "You're like a bowerbird."

"I gather them for a different purpose than a bowerbird does."

"You know what a bowerbird is?" said the man. "They don't live in this part of the world."

"I've seen them. I've seen the world through a thousand eyes," she said.

"I've seen a bit of the world too," he said. "Through my own."

"What's that thing around your ankle?" she asked.

"A thought-sliver," said the man. "It'll be gone in a minute or so."

The Bone Fisher had mentioned thought-slivers to his apprentice, mostly to complain about how they clogged the dream-weave. They were ephemeral, unimportant, so he said, but potentially dangerous to the untrained mind. The Bone Fisher had never let her handle one, or even see one close-to.

The apprentice was about to speak, to ask this man what he was doing with it, but he spoke before she did. "I'm Bellan, by the way. Hello. And good-bye." The thought-sliver disappeared like smoke and then he turned and in a peculiar gingerish run, he hurled himself up the slope of rolling pebbles and left her there on the beach.

The next time she saw Bellan, he was floating in the cove at dawn in a little coracle, like the ones she had seen the fishermen use, though none of the fishermen dared use this cove—it belonged to the Bone Fisher. And they never hunted for what the Bone Fisher caught.

Bellan stood in his coracle. "Hello, little Bowerbird," he said. He did not look up at her. He was too intent with what he was doing. He leaned over the edge of the boat with his hand outstretched over the water. He knew enough to find a calm patch of water, but he was clumsy and unskilled. When he thrust his hand into the water, he drew a splash, and he pulled up a thick ribbon of green that immediately turned bright pink and dissolved between his fingers. He swore and shook his hand. "That burned!"

"It would do," said the apprentice, "unless you fix it quickly."

Bellan put his hand in the water to cool it. "You know about these things?"

"Of course," she said. "I've been years learning them."

"Will you teach me?"

"Why?" she said.

"I want to learn. Will you teach me?"

"It would be dangerous."

Bellan paddled his coracle to the slipway where she stood and jumped out next to her. "I know a little," he said. "I've read about it, studied it. Most of the skills are practical though, and I need someone to show me."

The apprentice suspected what the Bone Fisher would do if he found anyone trespassing in his little cove, let alone angling for his knowledge. "The Bone Fisher would kill you," she said. "Eventually. But first he'd strip out your soul. You really shouldn't be here now. He could find out."

"He doesn't have to know."

He was a long time convincing her, and eventually, she agreed. She spent hours showing him how the lure was tossed so that it would twirl as it sank. She instructed him how to wait, leaning over the water until your back screamed at you, and longer until pain didn't matter. She taught him to cone his fingers before darting his hand into the water so as to break the surface silently. When he had learned all of these things well enough, she went out with him in his coracle and had him try. The first time he succeeded, he caught hold of a nightmare. He screamed and kept screaming long after she'd shaken it free of him and brought the boat aground. Afterwards, he cried like a small child, but he was still sane. He must be very strong of mind to have stood it and survived, she thought.

"That was awful," he said, wiping away tears.

"I know," she said. "I caught my mother's nightmare once. She dreams me as a monster seeking revenge. She thinks I have fins and fangs. The most hideous thing she's ever seen. She—"

"Stop it," said Bellan. "I can't stand it."

For a long time after that, the apprentice hardly saw Bellan, and when she did, he seemed reserved and cautious. Every time the apprentice went out onto the beach in search of lures, she looked for him. While on one of her trips, hoping for a sight of him, she found a little green crab in a tidal pool. Because there was room in the bucket, she filled it a little with water and put the crab inside and took it home. It became a fixture in her room. She put it into an old bucket and changed the water every day, and she took it out onto the beach with her and let it play on the sand. She had nothing else on which to lavish her affections. Lately on some days, the excess of feeling nearly drove her mad.

After a week of not seeing him at all, she set off across the sands when it was dark enough that no one would recognize her. She went into the little cove halfway along the pebbled beach and squeezed into the crevice in the rocks there. She wormed her way inside until she came to a little chamber. Here, she kept all of her possessions—hidden so the Bone Fisher wouldn't take them from her. She gathered the coins she had collected, found on the beach and hoarded over the years. She took all of them, half a hundred of them (she did not know how many she would need) and put them into her pocket. The other thing she took was the cloth mask she had found several years before. It was a rich piece of work, though the tiny jewels studding it were not on tightly and likely to be lost. It was a mask meant to cover the entire head, though hers being larger than most, it was tight to squeeze into. The mask was opulent, likely imported from another place. It was fashioned in the shape of an elephant with a long, baggy trunk that nearly trailed the ground. It had been cast onto the beach, as many masks were discarded on the Festival Night when the real celebrations began.

She donned this mask along with her usual clothes, and a pair of gloves, also found on the beach. She had stuffed the finger and thumb with rags so that no one would know she was lacking them.

For the first time in her life, she braved the company of other people. For the first time in her life, she had reason enough to brave the company of other people. Dressed as she was, she fit in amongst the contrived grotesquerie of the others. No one paid her any mind.

She was at first overwhelmed with the feeling of people, so many people around her. She was surprised at the warmth of their bodies, pressed against her in the crowds. She found it strange at first, then unpleasant, and she pushed and poked her way through to a less crowded place. She had thought that it would be easy to find him, that no matter how he was costumed, she would recognize him. But she had not imagined so many people, so many colors, so much clutter, so much *noise*. One little child, dressed like a monkey, took hold of her trunk and tried to swing from it. The apprentice had to snatch it away. She stopped to catch her breath, looking for a way of escape back to the beach, but she was blocked by columns of people, five- and six-deep. There was no escape, except behind her, where she found a scarlet tent with an opening large enough for her. She slipped inside. Here, it was quiet, and there were no crowds. Only one woman, sitting, waiting expectantly, not pressing herself onto her like the others.

"Tell your fortune, miss?" The woman indicated a large red cushion opposite.

The apprentice sat, and produced her bag of coins. She set them in front of the fortune-teller. The fortune-teller's eyes widened when she looked inside. She set the bag aside and said, "May I see your palm?"

The apprentice hesitated, and extended her hand.

The fortune-teller sighed and before the apprentice could protest, she had pulled off her glove, revealing her three-fingered hand. The fortune-teller sat in silence, looking at her hand, but she neither shrank from it, nor did she seem repulsed. And then the apprentice noticed that the other woman's throat was mottled with deep green skin beneath her twists of scarf. She was a monster too, though one who could pass for normal.

"Will you not read my fortune?" said the apprentice.

"I can see it quite plainly."

"What must I do to win him?"

The fortune-teller shook her head.

"Tell me," said the apprentice. "If I must wait. I can wait a lifetime."

"No," said the fortune-teller. "He will never love you that way. And if you continue to demand of him what he cannot give you, he will come to hate you."

"What can I do, then?"

"You can do nothing to change his mind," said the fortune-teller. "At least, not to turn it towards you. You have two options. The first is to go on as you are. You will live, possibly love another man. But you will not win that one either."

"How do you know?" said the apprentice.

"I have experience in these matters," said the fortune-teller.

"What's the second option?"

"To stop going on as you are."

"You mean… die?"

"Not necessarily," said the fortune-teller. "But you must change yourself somehow."

The apprentice went home with her thoughts. Crossing the beach, she stripped off the elephant mask and dropped it onto the sand. It had been one of her most prized possessions, but it had served its purpose.

The Bone Fisher had noticed that for some time now his apprentice had been eating less and less, toying listlessly with her food. Moreover she had been of late, morose and sullen. More of a concern, she had been bringing in fewer and fewer pieces of glass, which seemed odd as she seemed to be spending more and more time on the beach. She kept her secrets well, but he knew she must have some. He had always respected her sleep, all her life. He had protected her dreams, warded away the nightmares which would surely have preyed on her young mind, fed as it was with the worst memories he could find for her. Her dreams had, until now, been sacrosanct to him. But as he watched her from day to day wasting away in front of him, saying less and less, he decided that he must find out what the trouble was. So that night when he saw her coming back across the sands when she ought to have been sleeping, he waited until she did sleep and then he delved into her dreams. Straight away, he found Bellan in her memories. In fact, there was little else among her dreams but images of him. When she went out on the beach these days, she wasn't searching for glass, she was searching for her heart, watching for a lone figure on the lip of the tide. The Bone Fisher was surprised and somewhat revolted by his discovery, and he abandoned her to her pointless dreaming.

Who was Bellan? The name was a ghost in his memory, but then, he knew so many names. He knew everyone's names.

He went out in his seashell boat with the choicest pieces of glass, the palest green ones, in the quiet of pre-dawn, though the waters and dreams were more turbulent than he would have liked. They always were after the Night of Masks.

The Bone Fisher found Bellan after a bit of searching. For some reason, the young man's dreams were muted, quiet things. Not weak, but still and focused. Who was Bellan? Bellan had dreamed a thousand dreams in which he was the hero, in which he rescued children and the helpless from danger. This was not unusual, but about Bellan, there was plenty which was. In none of his dreams did the apprentice figure, nor any maiden, young, beautiful or otherwise. Nor could the Fisher find, as happened in some such cases, a desire for young men. There was simply no desire of that type for men or women in this man at all. And yet Bellan was neither innocent nor damaged. He was whole. He didn't love the apprentice at all, had no capacity to do so. The Fisher was disinclined to instill such desire in him, even had he known how it could be done. No, the Fisher's anger had dissipated at this revelation. He did not understand Bellan, but he was intrigued enough to let him sleep, at least another night, perhaps longer, so that he could study him.

The morning after the Night of Masks, while walking the beach and searching for Bellan, the apprentice contemplated her situation. How many days would she spend like this, yearning, suffering to no purpose? How much futile dreaming? Life had been pain enough before this, but it had been a quiet pain. Now, it roared so loudly she could hardly sleep, hardly think. Yet it was the noise of nothing, a complete fantasy. If the fortune-teller had counselled her correctly, she should stop going on the way she was. How, though? By ending her life? She suffered, but she did not want to die. She felt more alive now than she ever had before. What other way was there to change? The Bone Fisher might be able to do something. The Bone Fisher was a powerful man… would he deny her this one request?

As they sipped soup from the skulls of a married couple that evening, she said to the Bone Fisher, "I want my desire for love to die."

"Die?" said the Bone Fisher. He was a wise creature, experienced in worldly things, witness to the world's happiness and tragedies, in the ways of love (He had known it once himself, and it had left him bitter). But he had never encountered such a wish as this one, nor had he expected this request from her.

"I want my desire to go," she said. "I want you to take it away. I was happier without it. I want to stop wanting."

He had raised her to be strong, tough. He had not expected to be confronted with this cold practicality. A part of him felt suddenly very sad. "To take away your memory of him, you mean?" he said.

"No," she said. "I want to keep my memories. But I want them uncolored by this… this curse of wanting."

"To take away your hunger would kill you," he said. "To take away your appetite, you would have no will to eat."

"What I hunger for, I can live without," she insisted. "If I must live without it, I would rather not hunger for it too."

That she was damaged, inside as well as out, was clear. He could not heal her. He was no healer. But she was not asking him to heal her. She was asking him to break her even more until the inside no longer hurt. If that could be done.

The Bone Fisher nodded. He would try to grant her request, though he was not sure how he would do it.

He thought about it many days, and then one morning, he asked her to join him in his seashell boat. She had not ridden in this boat since the early days of her apprenticeship when he had first initiated her into the sickness of the world, guiding her through dreams and reality. She sat quietly in the stern, head bowed as though in thought, hands between her knees. She did not move or stir, though the water was rough in the bay, and it jostled the boat. She was very calm, now that she anticipated an end to her suffering.

The Fisher brought the boat into the cove. She stirred herself then and dropped the anchor, holding the mother-of-pearl gunwale to steady herself.

"Get into the water," he said to her.

She took off her shoes and did so. It was late in the fall, and the water was cold and black, but she knew how to swim, and he held her with his skeletal hand by the nape of her neck.

"I will have to hold you under for some time," he said. "You will struggle, but I will not let you go."

She was shivering too much to reply. The water was cold and silent, with a great emptiness below her. She glimpsed green ribbons some way beneath her and remembered Bellan pulling one free. Then the colors faded, and there was a great rumbling, as though the sea bed had opened, and she felt some of the warmth and the light, a pale-colored light, drawn out of her. The cold suddenly slipped into her. Instantly, she stopped shivering, lay limp while the Bone Fisher held her. She did not struggle, when he pulled her from the water and put her back in the bottom of the seashell boat. She lay in the boat, quiet now, not even shivering.

The Bone Fisher took off his cloak and lay it over her.

"I don't feel any different," she said, almost angrily. "Am I supposed to feel any different?"

Nor did she feel any different that night when she went to bed. Her dreams were empty, formless things, but then they always were on nights when the Bone Fisher didn't feed her, when she didn't tap the dreams.

On waking the next morning, she at first forgot that the night before had happened. Then she sat up, looked around her little room with its boots, rinsed in seawater and set in the corner upside down, her blue seashirt that she only wore on the windiest days. So ordinary, so normal, she wondered if she'd dreamed the day before, if today was the day of her surrender.

She went out onto the beach. It was later in the morning than she usually went. Perhaps that was why she saw Bellan, for he lately seemed to have been avoiding her. At first, she didn't recognize him, seeing a figure in a gray smock, paddling the coracle out by the point. It was him, and yet…the colors of the day were faded, the sea strange and flat, even the pebbles were like paper. She looked at him and looked at him. "I used to love him," she thought. She peered hard at him, trying to understand what that meant, but her keen eyes could not spot a whisper of charm, and she quickly grew bored. She had glass to collect. And indeed, the Bone Fisher noted as the days passed, that his apprentice brought in buckets heaping with glass, more than she ever had before, even though her trips to the beach became shorter.

One morning, she tipped out her bucket with her little green crab and left him on the beach for the tide to take away. She reached into her pocket and pulled out the golden locket with its grains of sand inside.

There are three kinds of people in the world.
Which one am I?
She threw the locket into the sea.

A Little Tea and Personal Magnetism

Things to do:
1. Ponder Purpose in Life. Must be Large and Important as Mummy always said I was destined for Great Things. Would like to be Brilliant Writer. Already *am* Brilliant Writer (Mummy said so) but would like Everyone to *know* am Brilliant Writer. Except, how?

The first thing you must do is to design an impressive business card.
—From: *How to Be a Brilliant Writer* by Mary Sue Chaparter

<s>George Yarmouth Whynot, Literary Wizard</s>
<s>George Yarmouth Whynot, Nobel laureate (Literature)</s>
<s>George Yarmouth Whynot, OBE</s>
George Y. Whynot, Wordsmith

Good. Except… Mummy said destined for Great Things, plural. So what else? Would like to help people. Many people helped = Me being noticed as Brilliant and Important. Grateful people name stadiums after me. And babies. But not ugly babies. Only good-looking babies. On second thoughts, all babies somewhat ugly. Perhaps could have youths named after me, after ugly phase complete. Brilliant.

George Y. Whynot, Wordsmith & Philanthropist

Not quite impressive enough. Would also like to do Brave Things so people will recognize innate heroic nature of Me. But only as sideline, until Novel becomes best-seller.

George Y. Whynot,
Wordsmith, Philanthropist & Occasional Lion (!) Tamer
By Appointment Only Tel. 0154 67889

Note to self: Needs photo, in profile. Pref. retouched to disguise nose flob.
Note to self: Would like to be blond in photo. Possible? And ~~naked~~
strikingly underclothed, yet elegant and faun-like, with no bits showing.
Note to self: With whip?
Ask Marianna to buy me the following:
1. Whip (must be long and suitable for Lion)
2. Mary Sue Chaparter™ genuine leather-bound WRITER'S
NOTEBOOK with cream-colored Paper and gold leaf Edging (for writing
The Great British Novel in)

Marianna Bitalot walked into George's office without knocking. "George," she said. "I've just now had the most peculiar telephone conversation with Sir Timothy Hatfield's secretary."

George did not look up from his desk as he painstakingly cut around a portrait of René Descartes with a pair of round-ended scissors. "Not now, Marianna. Can't you see I'm engaged in my décolletage?"

"Your what?"

"Though I have to say, I would be more engaged if I could just find a semi-nude portrait of René Descartes to cut out."

"I think you'll find it's découpage, not décolletage," said Marianna. "Unless there's something you haven't told me. What do you want with René Descartes anyway?"

"To paste portraits of him onto my business cards of course, to suggest the virility of, well, me. One must project a certain image when one is in my profession."

"I wasn't aware that you had a profession, George. Other than lolling about and being generally annoying."

"I'll have you know," said George, "that I have plenty of gentlemanly occupations clamoring for my attention." He slapped his scissors down on the desk by way of emphasis. Unfortunately this decisive gesture was undermined somewhat by the fact that his forefinger and thumb caught in the loops of the scissors, and he had to shake himself free of them.

"Which reminds me," said Marianna, "Sir Timothy's secretary is coming here tomorrow at four PM to talk to you about the facilities you'll be needing for containing a wild beast. Do you have any idea what that's about?"

"Oh that," said George. "I promised Sir Timothy that I would tame a lion as entertainment at his wife's garden party."

"Of course you did."

"Which means you will have to get up a taming ensemble for me by the end of the week. I shall need a whip. And a black cape, velvet naturally. And, um," George winced, "a bit of a lion as well. Where would one find a lion these days?"

"Africa."

"It might be a bit pricey to have one flown in. I was thinking along the lines of something in closer proximity."

"The zoo might have one or two."

"Ah. Do you suppose they would rent us one for an hour or two next Saturday afternoon?"

"I really couldn't say," said Marianna.

"Well do go and ask them," said George. "And be sure to get the lion's references. I think I shall need to start with a really forgiving sort of lion, otherwise things could go a bit pear-shaped."

Marianna had been George's personal assistant for nearly two months. She had been his cousin ever since he had been born twenty-four years previously. She was very nearly fed up with both positions. Marianna could be a formidable presence when put-upon. George really did not fully comprehend the dangerous ground on which he was treading. Marianna hated George with the kind of intense passion that kittens often reserve for small moving objects.

At times, you may find it necessary to convey to the reader large blocks of information important in the understanding of the story. When this happens, try not to draw the reader's attention to the fact that this is what you are doing. An effective trick is to distract them with a fascinating fact. For instance, did you know that the world's tallest free-standing structure is known to its closest friends as 'Herbert'? Now you do!

   —Babs Ketchen: *How to Infodump So No One Will Notice*

When Marianna returned from cape-shopping, she was greeted by George at his office door. "Marianna! I've got my first lion-taming job. Come and see!"

"What? In your office?" said Marianna.

"Yes! Come on!" George darted back into his office.

George was leaning over his desk, more specifically, over a cardboard box on his desk.

"George…?" said Marianna.

"Now," said George. He lifted the box to reveal, sitting underneath it, a small, black-and-white kitten.

"George—"

"This is my first lion," said George. "His name is Caligula."

"George, it's a kitten."

"It's an abbreviated lion substitute, Marianna." He uncoiled his whip.

"George, you are not going to hit that kitten."

"Oh, come on, Marianna, just a little."

Marianna's face hardened.

"It's only a small whip," said George. "I won't hit it very hard."

"You will not hit him at all," said Marianna, "or I will bloody well use *you* as a lion substitute."

"All right," said George. "Then you leave me no choice but to use my manly physical presence to cow it." He brandished the whip in the kitten's face. "Now look here, Caligula, I command you to yield to me."

The kitten began to lick itself.

"Ah ha. You see, Marianna? They always lick their manly bits when they're intimidated. I read it in a book. Stand back. I'm going to reinforce my dominance."

"Is that a mouse in the corner?" said Marianna.

George leapt onto his chair and screamed.

Marianna, succumbing to the inexorable attraction all spinsters possess in regard to kittens, picked up Caligula and left the office. In compliance with the Spinster Home Code she already had four cats, but in accordance with Section 2, subsection b, she did have emergency facilities to accommodate a fifth.

The second thing you must do is to tell everyone about your book, at every opportunity. This way, you will get noticed, and generate interest in your novel. Don't actually let them read it, though, otherwise they'll steal your ideas.

—Mary Sue Chaparter, Writer

“ “Sir Timothy's wife is very excited about your proposed entertainment for the garden party,” said Sir Timothy Hatfield's secretary. “It ought to bring in plenty of charitable donations. They've never seen a lion tamer before.”

“Nor have I,” said Marianna.

George cleared his throat. “Actually…the reason I called you to my office was to propose a slight tweak to the program. I thought that possibly, instead of the lion taming I could open the garden party with a lecture about my novel.”

“I didn't know you were a writer,” said the secretary.

“I prefer to think of myself as a 'Wordsmith',” said George.

“What books have you published?” said the secretary.

“Well…” said George, “None *as such*. But I'm in the process of thinking about writing one. I've done up the most *extraordinary* title page. It's got 'Booker Prize' written all over it. See?” He pointed to the title page, on which was written *Booker Prize* eleven times.

“…and in your handwriting, too,” said Marianna.

“Well, of course I did that myself; every little bit helps, you know. When you're creating a Masterpiece. What it really needs is more pictures, but I'm having trouble finding a semi-nude illustration to represent my hero. He has the handsome, chiseled features of a Sir Isaac Newton and the rugged body of a René Descartes. You can see my problem.”

“I think anyone could,” said Marianna.

“So… you haven't actually written this book?” said the secretary.

“Well, I've nearly started Chapter One. I've got the most brilliant idea for it. All of the people I've talked to about it have been astonished, I can tell you.”

“Who was astonished?” said Marianna.

“Oh, you know…” said George. “That man we met in the lift at Harrods. The one who mistook you for a man. He was there buying bolt cutters for his grand-niece in Canada. You remember.”

“He was drunk, George,” said Marianna.

“And what about Emily Binghamton…at the Binghamton's party? She wasn't drunk. I told her about it, and she loved it.”

“She threw her drink in your face.”

"Yes, you see," said George to the secretary. "That's because it astonished her so much—works of genius often do that."

"Look here," said the secretary. "I'm not sure about this book-thing of yours, but you *will* still be taming a lion for us?"

"Well…" said George, adjusting his tie. "You know I'd really love to, but my lion taming outfit is at the dry cleaners at the moment, and they're having the devil of a time getting the crème de menthe stains out. It sort of got a drink tossed onto it, with me in it."

"Emily Binghampton?" said the secretary.

"No, no. Completely different woman this time," said George.

"'This time'?" said the secretary. "How many women have thrown drinks at you?"

"What? The same woman?" said George.

"No. How many different women?"

"Oh… well," George laughed nervously. "Who keeps track of these things?"

"Seventeen," said Marianna. "Since April."

"The price we pay for Empire, eh?" said George. He laughed heartily.

"Look, Mr. Whynot," said the secretary. "I'm not at all sure about this change in the program. A lot of people are going to be very disappointed if the lion taming is canceled. They may well withdraw their support. As you know, this party is being held to raise money for the Guild of the Poor Dear Souls."

"Is it?" George's gaze slid to the corner of the room where the hole in the wainscoting was. He thought he'd heard a mouse. Whenever he was nervous, he generally thought he heard mice. Surreptitiously he lifted his feet off the floor and perched them on the edge of his chair. He hugged his knees to his chest.

"Really, Mr. Whynot, no one will mind if you wear an alternate costume so long as you're taming a lion. So can we count on you to deliver the goods?"

"You have my word as a gentleman and a lion tamer," said George.

"Excellent," said the secretary. He shook George's hand and left.

"You're in for it now, George," said Marianna.

"I am *not*," said George.

"So you're actually going to tame a lion this weekend, then?" said Marianna.

"Never mind the lion," said George. "I've just thought of an alternate plan."

"And what's that?"

"I am going to convert a charwoman."

"Of course you are," said Marianna. "Why, exactly?"

"Simple, Marianna. If I produce a converted charwoman at the Hatfield's garden party, everyone will be so mightily impressed with my act of philanthropy that they'll forget all about the lion taming."

"Ah," said Marianna. "And where are you going to get a converted charwoman?"

"I'll make one from an unconverted charwoman," said George. "Hector Munro says you can turn them by fifties with a little tea and personal magnetism."

"You can rescue charwomen by fifties with a little tea and personal magnetism."
—H.H. Munro (Saki) (1904)

"We have the ingredients," George continued. "You shall supply the tea, and I, of course, shall supply the magnetism. I think we can agree that I've got heaps of magnetism."

"Spadefuls, even," said Marianna.

"Right," said George. "Now, go and get me a charwoman and bring her here."

"How exactly would I do that?" said Marianna.

George snapped his fingers. "Look one up in the book."

"The book?"

"There must be a book out there on the subject. The Book of English Charwomen or something. Like a Debrett's for the working class."

Your hero needs to be handsome, charming, intelligent and just BIG *at everything. Especially* when it comes to the opposite sex!
—Mary Sue Chaparter

"What a great fibber that Hector Munro was!" said George, regarding the large tea stain on his suit jacket. "Charwoman are *not* easy to convert at all. That Mrs. Dingle wasn't at all impressed by my obvious charm."

"I don't think your comments about her breasts went over well," said Marianna.

"Didn't they?" said George, sounding surprised.

"No. And just for future reference, women's breasts are not detachable."

"Are you *sure*?" said George.

"I would know, George."

"Well, of course, you *would* say that, wouldn't you? It's all part of the sisterhood secrecy pact."

As a matter of fact, George had never fully grasped the point of a woman's 'bosoms.' They looked faintly ridiculous to him. He had long suspected that when women got together in private, they would take their bosoms off, waggle them around and have a good laugh. Or sometimes slap each other about with them in lieu of a pillow fight. In fact, George deduced, women only bothered to carry them around in order to distract men with their general silliness of shape and gelatinous texture. This was the great secret that all women kept and that George, alone among men, had managed to suss out.

"I expect you keep yours in your top drawer at night," said George to Marianna.

Some days, the appeal of familial homicide was almost overwhelming for Marianna.

"Marianna, take my jacket to the dry cleaners and see if they can get the tea stains out. I think I ought to qualify for a volume discount. Or maybe I can write it off as a business expense."

"What are you going to do about the party, George?"

"There's nothing for it; I shall have to finish writing my novel, get it published by Saturday, and then I can safely give a reading of it at the Hatfield's garden party."

"Right," said Marianna. "Good luck."

10:00 AM: Needs BIGGER LETTERS. Must look Imposing and Deep or people won't take me SERIOUSLY as a Writer.

The Price They Paid For Empire:
(the Great British Novel)
by
George Y. Whynot
BOOKER PRIZE WINNER!!

12:00 noon: much better. Ah, lunch: watercress sandwiches—must maintain my sleek, manly physique. And a few glasses of Château de Boeuf, to maintain the mindset of the tortured artist.
2:00 PM: back to work!

Always begin your novel with a statement of such profundity that it will leave your reader in wonder at your genius.

—Mary Sue Chaptarter, Writer

Chapter One

The sea was wet and full of olives.

2:05 PM: Hmmm, then what? Stuck.
2:15 PM: Still stuck.
2:20 PM: *Still* stuck. Must have writer's block.

George threw down his pen and burst out into reception. "That's it, Marianna! I'm blocked! Hopelessly stuck."

Marianna whipped her latest bodice-ripper into the bottom drawer of her desk and slammed it closed.

"There's nothing for it," said George, gripping the edges of her desk. "I shall have to go on a Writer's Retreat."

"A writer's retreat?"

"Yes. All the great authors went on them. Mandy Sommet went to Ninian Park. Mary Sue Chaparter went to Mold. And I shall go to the Gulf of Auden."

"There is no such place as the Gulf of Auden, George."

"Of course there is, Marianna! I was *born* in the Gulf of Auden."

"You were born in Splott," said Marianna. "Your mother called it the Gulf of Auden to sound posh."

"Nonsense, Marianna. Mother told me all about the G. of A.:

> Where peacocks frolic
> and quince trees abound,
> and emergency brains
> spring from the ground.

"There's a lake filled entirely with Château de Boeuf and a boatman made of pressed sugar. He isn't real, of course, but the sugar is, and you can lick him if you're so inclined."

"George, you haven't got time to go on a writer's retreat to Splott or anywhere else. You've got the garden party tomorrow. You're supposed to be taming a lion."

"Can't you just tell Sir Hatfield that I've gone on an emergency lion-taming mission in the Gulf of Auden?"

"I will not tell lies for you," said Marianna. "Not without a significant raise in pay."

"Oh, right," said George. He adjusted his tie "Well, um… that's a bit of a tricky one then."

"What are you going to do?"

"You'd better drum me up a lion impersonator."

"Lion impersonator?" said Marianna.

"You know, something approximately lion-sized, but not particularly dangerous."

On the day of the garden party, George found himself drawn to a charity stall displaying arts and crafts for sale in aid of the Poor Dear Souls Guild. George took an immediate interest in some scrapbooks made from illustrations of Victorian children's books. Twelve-year old Canadian schoolgirl, Miss Paula Pace-Kettering was manning the stall.

"Do you have any books with portraits of Sir Isaac Newton?" George asked.

"No," said Paula, "but this one's got some Arthur Conan Doyle-authenticated fairies."

"I must say," said George to her, I do have a particular fondness for fairies."

Paula giggled. Paula's aunt, sensing a potential sale in the offing, drifted over towards them.

"May I help you?" she said to George.

"Oh no," said George, "not at all. I was just admiring your niece's décolletage."

"I beg your pardon!?" said Mrs. Kettering.

"It's all right, Auntie Beryl," said Paula. "He's gay."

"I'm… what?" said George. "Now look here, young lady, just because I can tell that Sir Isaac Newton is an incredibly handsome man, and I like cut-out pictures of fairies does not render me some kind of… of…." George made a fussy gesture with his hands. "I'd rather lick a mouse than make romantic overtures towards a man—even Sir Isaac!"

"Paula, go and help your mother in the tea tent," said Beryl Kettering. She shot a steely look at George which sent him backing away hastily, readying himself to duck should any teacups, collectable teaspoons or fairy books happen to be flung at him.

As Mrs. Kettering was fingering one of the heavier scrapbooks, George beat a hasty retreat to the nearest enclosed space he could find, which happened to be the chapel on the grounds of the Hatfield's estate.

George was not immense with churches. His mother practiced atheism religiously and had kept him enraptured throughout his formative years (which were still ongoing) with terrifying tales which she claimed to be of biblical origin, but which were actually complete fibs.

George's trepidation on entering the church stemmed from a larger concern, though. As everyone knows, churches are notorious for containing mice. George was even less immense with mice than he was with churches hence, until now he had never set foot in one. Upon entering the chapel, therefore, George immediately vaulted onto an empty pew and nervously scanned the floor. At this point, he noticed that he was being watched. A man was standing nearby looking solemn.

"Hello?" said George. "You're not a… a saint of some sort, are you?"

"I'm the Archdeacon."

"Ah," said George.

"Are you going to come down?" said the Archdeacon.

"I can see everything quite nicely from here, thanks," said George. "For instance that… flat wooden thing over there. I can see that perfectly."

"The altar."

"Oh yes, the altar," said George, assuming an air of authority. "I imagine you have to scrub it quite hard to get the bloodstains off."

"Bloodstains?"

"From the sacrificial goats."

"What?" said the Archdeacon. "No one sacrifices goats in here."

"Oh, well no, not *nowadays*," said George. "Too unsanitary. Of course they do it out the back and then they bring the blood into the church in a thermos. Modern times, eh?"

"What are you doing up there?"

"Avoiding the mice." George gave a little shudder. "They run up one's trouser legs and make themselves at home in one's most intimate places, and I *will not have it!*" He directed this last to the church in general, for the benefit of any nearby murine ears.

"I've never seen any mice in here," said the Archdeacon.

"Of course you wouldn't. They camouflage themselves for stealth. Stained glass pelts so you don't see them coming."

A few moments of awkward silence followed.

"Of course," said George, "you and I are in somewhat of the same line of work."

"Oh, yes?"

"I'm a philanthropist," said George.

"Oh, yes? In what capacity?"

"Well," said George, adjusting his tie. "People come to me with their problems, and I help them. Ish. This past week, for instance, I converted a charwoman."

"Really?" said the Archdeacon.

"Well, nearly. *Very* nearly. I would have done, but for a small misunderstanding about her breasts. Apparently they don't come off."

"How interesting." The Archdeacon glanced quickly over his shoulder. "Excuse me. My wife is trying to catch my attention." He then made a swift exit, passing Paula Pace-Kettering at the entranceway of the chapel.

"Hello?" said Paula. She made her way to the front of the chapel where George was still perched on the edge of the pew.

"Hello," said George. "Your aunt—"

"I ditched her. Look, I'm sorry I called you a fairy earlier."

"Oh no, not at all," said George. "I'm not, though."

"Come down, would you?" Paula coaxed George down from the pew by dint of tugging sharply on his tie and causing him to lose his balance.

George got up and dusted himself off. "Your aunt seemed quite het up back there."

"It was that comment you made about my décolletage."

"What about it? I was being charming, admiring your scrapbooks."

"That's découpage—cutting things out with paper and gluing them onto a backing."

"Well what on Earth's décolletage, then?"

Paula smirked, unbuttoned the top two buttons on George's shirt, hooked her finger in and looked down. She winked at him and left the chapel.

George blushed and clutched his shirt closed.

"Mr. Whynot!" called a voice in the distance. Sir Timothy's secretary stood at the chapel door gesturing for his attention.

George dove under a pew like a meerkat that's spotted an owl.

The footsteps grew closer and George felt himself being shaken. "Mr. Whynot! Your lion has arrived."

"Er…" said George.

"Come on, we're all waiting for you in the pavilion." He hauled George to his feet and despite George's making windmill motions with his arms, managed to drag him out to the middle of the lawn where a large, red-and-white striped pavilion had been put up.

If we could see into George's mind we would discover that these are the things that George is most afraid of, listed in ascending order of terror:

1. Mice
2. Death
3. Bosoms
4. Losing face

George dug his heels into the soft grass of the croquet lawn and brought himself to a halt. "I can't possibly tame a lion now," he said.

"Why not?"

"Because… well for a start, I haven't got my whip."

"Your personal assistant has brought it for you along with your cape."

The secretary manhandled George inside the pavilion. There, a large, velvet-draped cage stood in the middle of an enclosure, ringed by a crowd of people. Among them stood Marianna carrying a coiled whip and a cape. When she saw George, she relieved the secretary of his charge and pulled George aside. She handed him his whip and buttoned on his cape.

"I won't have it, Marianna," said George. "I will not go in there with a lion. My death would be a tremendous loss to Society, not to mention the World of Literature."

"It's not a lion," Marianna whispered. "The zoo didn't have any. The closest they could manage was a honey badger."

"Right," said George. "Does a honey badger look lion-ish?"

"Not particularly, but for the sum of £20, they agreed to drape a lion skin over it."

"Right," said George. "Um… are they dangerous?"

"According to the leaflet the zookeeper gave me, they eat honey."

"That's all?"

"He allowed that they would also eat the occasional human scrotum, but only in special circumstances."

"I will not have my manly bits endangered, Marianna. The future of the British Empire rests almost entirely on the manly bits of men like me."

"I consider this a service to my country, then," said Marianna, and she pushed George through the gate and into the enclosure.

George stood trembling at one end of the enclosure furthest from the covered cage. The crowd applauded politely. Marianna hurried to the other end of the enclosure and, using a rope and pulley, hoisted the velvet covering from the honey badger's cage. The sides of the cage were hinged to fall away when its roof was removed and this was what they did, causing George to jump slightly.

The honey badger had recently been fed, and was a much smaller and less intimidating specimen than George had expected. Its body was concealed under a rather moth-eaten lion skin from which its head protruded. It appeared to be dozing.

In this time of crisis, George found that the sum total of his heritage in the form of generations of Whynots, manifested itself in a single, Great Idea: He would sneak up on the sleeping badger, carefully place his foot on its furry belly in a pose of conquest, have his photo taken and then remove himself from the enclosure, post-haste. It was a wonderful plan, and it would have worked. Had not, at the moment of truth as George held his foot poised over the belly of his conquest, the badger opened its eye and looked at him.

Animals possess a natural ability to detect fear. They also have that innate ability to differentiate between someone who is trying to tame one due to an excess of bravado, and someone who is doing it in order to live up to the wild claims on his business card.

There is a common piece of wisdom thrown about on the subject and that is, that if you see an angry lion approaching you, you should run away. This is nonsense. The best course of action, in this case, is to fling Christians at it.

—Capitulus Primus (from: *Lion Taming Made Easy*)

George had only a split second to react. He bounded over the honey badger (achieving a height which would have stunned his Physical Education teacher at school) and launched himself straight into the mass of party-goers gathered at the edge of the enclosure. His entrance into the crowd was accompanied by a startled exclamation, and he found himself face to face with the Archdeacon. George found that the most useful thing about Archdeacons was that one could hide behind them in times of need. Honey badgers, or at least this one, seemed to find them more attractive too.

As George dove behind the Archdeacon, he heard a most unfortunate scream behind him.

Philanthropist Throws Archdeacon
To Lion Stand-In
Whynot, Indeed!
(details on page 3)

"Yes, I know it's a bit of a mess," said Mr. George Whynot, Philanthropist and Lion Tamer, "but try to see it from my point of view. Clearly, the zoo was at fault for providing me with incomplete information regarding honey badger feeding habits. They ought to have said, 'eats honey, occasional manly bits and Archdeacons.' This all could have been avoided with a properly worded leaflet."

Never forget to end your masterpiece on a deep and profound note. Reflect on the Human Condition, if possible.

—Mary Sue Chaparter

"Marianna?" said George. "Do the think the dry cleaners know how to remove bits of Archdeacon from a velvet cape?"

The Teasewater Five

Published in *The Nine Muses*, 2005.
Honorable Mention, *Year's Best Fantasy and Horror*, 2006.

Miss Anna-Lisa Evans went by that name all her life. Marriage never arrived to alter it and when she had her only son she saw no reason why he shouldn't bear it also. Even on such a short journey. Thus, he was buried, three days after his birth, under a stone marked 'Midway Evans.' She'd called him Midway on first discovering her pregnancy as she'd declared his mere existence as "midway to ruining my reputation"; having a child out of wedlock in that era was not looked well upon. The boy's arrival as a stillborn fairly completed the journey, as it took the delicate edge of her eccentricity and twisted it like a Celtic knot.

From the hospital, Anna-Lisa retreated to the house in Telltale Close which she shared with her bachelor brother, Marlow. Here she resumed her occupation as a model-maker and freelance illustrator, busying herself pinning insects and tramping along hedgerows at dawn, eavesdropping on birds. None of which were unusual activities for her. However, the character of her paintings began to shift subtly from realism to surrealism.

A request to draw a likeness of an indigo bunting was met with pictures of the striking bird in various odd and improbable circumstances: drinking tea at a table on the patio, or sitting on the wrist of a cherubic child. A commission for a spotted salamander was duly filled, but rather than posed in its natural habitat, the gormless creature was pictured clutched in the hand of same cherubic child.

Her brother, Marlow, spent most of his tidy life successfully avoiding reality by using his unique gifts to simulate it as nearly as possible. At first he coped with his sister's growing obsession by ignoring it, but eventually the unsold artwork began to spill out of her studio and into his life. He found one of her paintings gracing the bottom of the bathtub one evening. Nor was this to be an isolated occurrance. Scattered over the kitchen table at breakfast the next morning, he found several more. All of them featured, in one pose or another, the same young child with golden, curling hair and overlarge blue eyes that hadn't quite settled comfortably in his fleshy face. In one picture, he held a meadow vole in his cupped hands. In another, a frog drooped, its grotesquely long legs hanging and dripping from his hand as he stood, knee-deep in pondwater.

Marlow was emotionally stunted in many ways, but he wasn't obtuse. He knew well enough that the inspiration for these sad paintings lay under several feet of cold topsoil in the Teasewater Cemetary. Marlow had always wanted a son, in the vague, wistful way that middle-aged bachelors with no experience of actual children sometimes did. In his idealized imagination, children appeared only when necessary, when surnames and heavy parcels were to be carried, while at other times they became unobtrusive, feeding, clothing and amusing themselves. In his own way, Marlow had been happily anticipating the birth of Anna-Lisa's child. Who else would have looked after them in old age and inherited the family fortune?

Marlow was concerned for Anna-Lisa, but also at a loss as to what to do about her. He reasoned that in time, her grief would lessen and life would resume in its own quiet way. But as the months passed, the paintings and sketches began to multiply. Marlow noticed a difference in these newer drawings. Though the animals never completely disappeared, they were no longer the focus. And the cherubic child was aging unnaturally swiftly. He had shed the androgenous appearance of infancy and was now clearly recognizable as a boy; his hair had darkened to a deep bronze, though it was still curling. The eyes looked less out of proportion in the face which had shed the chubbiness of babyhood. When he smiled now, a tooth, slightly twisted, showed beneath his upper lip. One of his eyebrows was completely white; his newt-slender fingers sported gnawed-on nubs of fingernails. In one drawing, he stood with one foot balanced on a broken tree stump half-submerged by the bank of a river, playing out a fishing line that ran into the water—no rod, just a line—and watching intently. This picture, Marlow took up to his bedroom and placed on the top of his bureau. He was not one for pretty pictures, but this one, he thought, was worth keeping. It provoked troubling questions in him. What if Midway—silly name, really—hadn't died? What if he had come home to the house and they had raised him? What kind of man would he have become?

Marlow roused himself from his reverie and, feeling somewhat overcome by a motive he didn't want to analyze too closely, he put on his coat and went for a walk. He chose a route that took him through the park. It was that time of day when most people were at work and their children at school—Marlow's preferred time to walk. Of late, he had found that seeing children bothered him a great deal. It had been weeks since he had seen a real child. But this day must have been a school holiday, because they were everywhere. The wind was gusting in the playing field at the park. Marlow saw a young boy running in circles tugging a kite string while his mother, a young woman, yelled encouragement. The boy was intently hauling on the string, and there was a look of joy on the mother's face. Marlow stood on the pathway watching them, his head full of the roar of the wind.

He returned home, if anything, more agitated than when he had left. He sought solace in his workshop. Lately he had been working on a life-sized damselfly. Anna-Lisa had designed the model so that it was impossible to distinguish it with its bead-blue body and clear wings, from a real damselfly. Most of her models she sold to universities, schools and museums. But in this particular case, Marlow, seeing what she had done, had asked that she make one for him. He had it in mind to push the envelope in his imitation of nature. He had been designing intricate machinery within the body to allow the damselfly to not only fly, but also catch mosquitoes. And so far, he had succeeded. Now, he was improving on nature; he was designing her to recognize and hover near one particular person. Better than insect repellent, this jewel-bodied servant would be.

When Marlow finally killed the lights above his workbench, it was well after midnight. On his way to bed, he passed Anna-Lisa's studio and found the door open and the lights still burning. Inside, Anna-Lisa was working at her dissecting microscope. She used this for illustrating smaller specimens, mostly insects. Tonight, though, she was not illustrating; she was sculpting another model, and there was a particular intensity in her expression, like the boy in the park with the kite, as though what she was doing hurt her more than it hurt the modelling medium. She was plying it with a sharp instrument, and Marlow was reluctant to interrupt, so he went to bed.

The next morning found Anna-Lisa drinking tea in the kitchen and chewing her toast distractedly. It put Marlow in mind of the days before Midway, peaceful, contented mornings when they would eat breakfast and discuss their various projects or plan collaborations.

"You're up early," said Marlow.

"I haven't been to bed yet," she said. "Come and look what I've done."

She led him upstairs, not to her workshop, but to the room at the end of the hall that had been locked for nearly a year. Despite the passage of time and the now open windows, it still smelt of fresh paint. In the sunlight, the room was bright with the wallpaper Marlow had put up in preparation for the baby who had never come home. Midway's father, whoever he was, had been either indifferent to Anna-Lisa's condition, or more likely, had never known of it. There had been no question of raising Midway anywhere but here in Telltale Close.

"It hasn't dried yet," said Anna-Lisa, leading him to the window by the crib.

Sitting on the sill was one of Anna-Lisa's model animals. This particular one lacked the realism that all of her previous creations possessed. Though it was recognizable as a meadow vole, it stood on its hind feet, exposing its gray belly. Its almost human expression was one of musing, as though the dead flies on the sill held its entire interest.

"Well?" said Anna-Lisa.

"What's it called?" Marlow asked.

"*He* is the Teasewater Vole," she said.

"He's… perfect," said Marlow.

"Not yet," said Anna-Lisa with a meaningful look.

No. What he lacked was spark inside. Marlow had, in a way, been saving himself for a challenge like this. Anna-Lisa was not asking him to make the creature simulate nature; she was asking him to give it something which nature could never do.

"You read my mind," said Marlow.

Both of them laughed, and their bodies and spirits, so unused to feeling joy for so long, ached with it.

After the Teasewater Vole came the Teasewater Otter—who carried a fishing pole and a pipe. Then the Teasewater Frog (a spring peeper with an ornate 'x' on its back). And finally, the Bird of Teasewater—an indigo bunting, the only bird mad enough to sing on a midsummer afternoon. In all, the work took Anna-Lisa two months. When the last stroke of blue had been made on the Bunting, she took him to the nursery and set him to dry on the wooden board in the window. She parted the curtains, letting the sun into the room.

Outside, the red maple tree enclosed the house in its wine-tinted light. She had chosen this room to be the nursery for its view of the trees in Telltale Close. The back garden was wild scrubland with none of the Close's majestic feel. What a world was outside, she thought; she had not properly looked at it in so long.

"Left a bit. Left a bit. There." The Bird of Teasewater perched on the arm of Marlow's desk lamp, peering down at him, giving him unsolicited directions. The Teasewater Otter lay on its back, spreadeagled on a wax-bottomed dissection tray while Marlow adjusted its voice box. He'd learned with the Bunting, having fitted him with a syrinx, the bird's equivalent of a larynx in mammals. If the Bunting was capable of speech and song, Marlow thought, why on earth shouldn't the Otter be as well? It wasn't as if he were compelled to follow nature's design; the Otter's miniature size, (it was a mere four inches in length) to Marlow's mind gave him license to tweak nature's nose. As he was doing so, a soft hum filled the room as the damselfly flitted in. The Bunting cocked his head at her.

"Leave her!" said Marlow. "Or I'll clip your wings."

The Bunting peered at Marlow and gave a gesture reminiscent of a shrug. Marlow suppressed a smile and went back to work.

Later, as he prepared lunch, he heard the front door click shut and looked up to see Anna-Lisa taking off her coat.

"You've been out," he said, surprised. Apart from her bird-watching excursions at the crack of dawn, he had not seen her leave the house since Midway's funeral.

In answer, she gave him a sly look and held up a white shopping bag. She pushed his plate aside, put the bag on the kitchen table and reached inside. She brought out an ebony case, the size of a briefcase with three silver clasps in the shape of mouse heads. The case was inlaid with silver and set with an amber locket in the middle of the lid. Inside the locket was a key. With the air of a magician's assistant, Anna-Lisa unlocked the case and lifted the lid. Inside, the case was… empty, but in quite an interesting way.

Anna-Lisa pulled back the green baize flaps in the lid to reveal a compartment within. Set in the foam lining were silk-trimmed burrows the size of egg cups crossed with straps like seatbelts. Beneath each one was a hand-lettered nameplate. At the very top, the same flowing script engraved on a plaque proclaimed: *The Teasewater Quintet.*

Anna-Lisa, still smiling, still silent, pulled back the black velvet cloth covering the bottom of the case. Under it was a landscape that Marlow recognized as a scale model of the grounds behind the house. The creek was represented by a piece of mirror cut in a serpentine shape; the grass and flowers of the banks were suggested with delicate dabs of paint. Some colored pebbles had been glued along the banks to represent boulders and a willow made of blown glass hung over the creek, its long icicle branches almost touching the mirror.

"It's a better place for them to sleep than in your drawer," she said with a trace of pride. She left the case on the table and went upstairs.

Marlow took the case downstairs. Pulling the lightswitch in the workshop, he was greeted by the song of the Bunting. He'd forgotten to shut it off. The rest of the menagerie, he pulled out of his fittings drawer.

It was only as he was placing them in their silk-lined burrows, buttoning the straps across to hold them in—Otter, Peeper, Vole, and Bunting—that he realized: *Quintet means five.*

Upstairs in her workroom, Anna-Lisa peered through the eyepieces of her dissecting microscope creating what was to be her masterpiece. The animals were wonderful, but they had been mere flirtations.

Permitting neither food nor sleep to interrupt the flow, she allowed her hands to move as though by divine force. So the time passed until at last she sat back from the bench, finished. In a daze, she took the figurine from the stage below the lenses and brought it to the nursery. She was so tired, she stumbled into the doorframe, but her work was protected from harm in her cupped hands. She opened the nursery window, set the piece in the window well and immediately sought her bed. Through that night and all the next day, she slept.

On the evening of the fourth day, Anna-Lisa awoke terribly thirsty and dizzy with hunger. She cupped water from the bedroom sink and took a few swallows. Then she remembered why she had slept for so long. She hurried to the nursery. The curtains lifted gently in a whisper of summer breeze. She parted them and picked up the figurine. She found details she did not remember putting there. It was as though someone else's hands had made him, not hers. She took him back to her room and peered at him under the microscope. His blond hair, tangled as though he had slept on it, (much as her own must look) the short upper lip under which his twisted incisor gleamed. His eyes had lost their babyish hue and were now a metallic yellow-brown. The white-browed eye looked naked. He stood no taller than a hen's egg, with the slight build of young adolescence. He was absolutely perfect. For the first time in a long time, the world seemed right again.

Marlow had a different opinion. He sat chewing his dinner and staring at the boy next to his plate. He showed no surprise, and made no move to touch the figurine, nor would he meet Anna-Lisa's eyes with their look of pleading hope.

"No," he said.

"Why not?"

"Because," said Marlow, and hearing the anger in his voice, he softened it. "It isn't real."

"Then what harm can it do…?"

"The same harm as any lie," he said.

"Would you turn your back on someone who needs you?" Her cupped hand hovered over the figurine as though to coax it toward him.

When Marlow didn't answer, she sighed and left the room leaving the figurine behind. Marlow set down his fork. He donned his reading glasses and, without touching the figure, examined it. She had sewn clothes for him out of scraps of fabric; he wore a matching blue shirt and trousers. She had outdone herself this time, he thought. The detail was so fine, so lifelike, he looked a breath and a twitch from animation. The boy seemed to stare at Marlow with reproach, the expectation of life implicit in his bearing. Marlow *could* do it. But should he?

"No," said Marlow firmly. He draped his napkin over the figurine and continued to eat. When he had finished, he picked the figurine up, still wrapped in the napkin and took it to the Teasewater case. He lay the boy in the empty foam burrow. It was only then he noticed the words on the plaque beneath the burrow: *Midway Evans*.

Anna-Lisa didn't beg or plead with Marlow. That wasn't her way. Instead, she withdrew to her room, emerging only to glean food from the kitchen. The lustre and life in her, rekindled momentarily with the creation of the figurine was now fading.

At first, Marlow thought it was simply the final and necessary stage of the grieving process. Acceptance. But it became clear as weeks passed that Anna-Lisa had entered a different stage altogether—apathy, the kind of apathy that preceeds the end of a terminal illness.

It was a coercion of the gentlest and most inexorable kind. If the alternative was her premature death, was granting her this wish, however illusory and false, not a kindness? Was false hope worse than no hope? These thoughts, along with the memory of the figurine's reproachful eyes, haunted Marlow. Had she indeed caught the merest trace of resemblance with the baby who had left her womb in silence?

Marlow decided at last, waking late one night from a dream of those eyes. Before he could change his mind in the light of morning, he took the case to his workshop. Brimming with excess energy, he almost expected the figure to come alive at his touch.

There was more to it than that, of course. And Marlow found himself contemplating the concept of a human soul, examining it as though it were under his own lenses and he were fumbling with it like a wet fish. Marlow was a recluse. He had no deep understanding of anyone other than himself. He had no one else to draw from.

Anna-Lisa's workmanship on the figure was exceptional. Breathtaking even. Marlow must do no less than match it. The Bunting had been his crowning achievement. Until now.

It took him four days, four glorious, tooth-grinding, frustrating, anxious days channelling the life that burned within him into the figurine. It was more than just his mind which he shared; it was his soul, his memories, all of it, melded with his sister's own essence which she had poured into its body. When it was over, Marlow felt the boy stir in his palm. He noted the movements of its belly as it breathed deeply, as though to fill itself to bursting, and felt a stab of triumph.

Marlow took the boy upstairs, wanting to see him in sunlight. On an impulse, he picked up the case from the living room and took it into the conservatory. He opened it. At the edge of the case, on the surface of the glass creek rested a tidy little rowboat. A pair of swizzel stick oars lay shipped inside. Marlow set the boy in the boat. The boy slumped there, limp, head bowed, still breathing deeply. After a time, his hands found the oar handles and he gripped them. He lifted his head, blinked and then peered over the side of the boat. He tapped the surface of the mirror with his oar experimentally, then looked up at Marlow.

"Who are you?" said the boy.

"Your… uncle, I suppose you could say. Uncle Marlow."

Midway shipped the oars and braced his bare feet, one on each of the oarlocks. "I need a proper pair of shoes," he said.

"Right," said Marlow. "I'll have your mother make you some."

"Is this all?"

"Is what all?" said Marlow.

"This!" He gestured, wide-armed, at the contents of the case. "I'm bored already."

"Right, I'll… wait a minute." Marlow opened the flaps in the lid and considered for a moment or two. The Bunting was likely to have a jealous sulk, the Vole to bore the boy rigid with his theories on religion, the Peeper was too small. So Marlow chose the Teasewater Otter. They were comparably sized at least, which Marlow, remembering his childhood days, believed to be the primary requisite of a suitable companion. In other words, someone unlikely to beat one senseless, and vice versa.

Marlow animated the Otter and set him on the dock next to the boat. The Otter immediately cast his fishing line into the creek. "Cheers," said the Otter.

"You're not going to catch any fish in that mirror, I hate to tell you," said Midway.

"Catching fish is not the reason I go fishing, young man," said the Otter. "I find it stimulates my imagination."

"It would have to. Reality's got sod-all to offer."

Marlow, satisfied they'd struck up some kind of rapport, however tenuous, went to the liquor cabinet across the room and poured himself a double scotch. He gulped it in three swallows and poured himself another. *Was I angry when I was working on him?* he thought. *Resentful? Cocky?*

Two drinks later, Marlow recalled that the boy didn't have an off switch. Hopefully, he would need sleep. Or at least pretend he did, for Marlow's sake.

"Right, ah, lights-out time, boys," said Marlow. He let the Otter reel in his line before deactivating him, then, hesitating, he picked up the boy and set him in his silk-lined bed. As an afterthought, Marlow tucked his hankerchief around the boy.

"I'm tolerating this under duress," said Midway.

Marlow bit back a curse. He oughtn't to swear in front of the boy. "Try to sleep," he said, and he made sure the straps keeping the boy in were buttoned securely. Then he closed the case, flicked the clasps and for the first time, he locked it with the key. He took the case up to his bedroom and stared at it for hours in a daze before sleep finally overcame him.

The next morning, Marlow took the case down to the kitchen and put it on the table, still locked. He was apprehensive about opening it, so apprehensive that he left it there and went to his workshop where he spent an hour twirling a pencil and staring off into space. When he went upstairs, he found Anna-Lisa sitting at the table, case open before her. She looked up and smiled a rare, radiant smile.

"He's perfect, isn't he, Marlow?"

Marlow had the power to shatter her hope by telling her what he thought. And he couldn't do it, because he saw in the sunlight that the hollows around her eyes were deep and her cheekbones sharp beneath her skin. Though she was only forty, she looked old. She could not take another devastating blow. So he said, "I suppose so."

"He wants a pair of binoculars for his birthday," said Anna-Lisa, "which would be today of course. And I'm going to make him a proper wardrobe. I'll get my sewing box. Watch him, would you?"

Midway balanced himself in the boat which bobbed in the kitchen sink. He was training his binoculars upwards at the curtain rail where the Bunting was perched.

"I can see *right* up your vent," said Midway cheerfully.

"Bloody twitcher," said the Bunting.

The Peeper, sitting opposite Midway in the boat, cocked his head and chipped in his high soprano. "What did he have for breakfast, then?"

"Eggs," said Midway. "Hard-boiled by the looks."

"Now look here," said Marlow. "Any more of that and I'll let the water out of the sink."

Across the kitchen table, Anna-Lisa held a piece of black velvet under a thimbled finger as she put the sewing needle through it. She went at the work with a blissful air.

This morning, Midway sported a suit of royal blue velvet. His boots were ungainly things, draw-string bags made out of muslin. They came up to his knees. The boy looked like a fop in them.

"Hasn't he got seven outfits already?" said Marlow.

"This is for the Peeper," said Anna-Lisa. "And I'm doing up a shawl for the Bunting next." She noticed Marlow's expression. "Why not?"

"It's biologically preposterous," he said. "Animals don't wear clothes."

"You're the one who made them able to speak," she said. "That wasn't my idea."

"I'm thinking that might have been a mistake."

"No," she said. "You'll leave them be. They're Midway's friends now."

"Look, lads," said Midway. "Lover's tiff."

Marlow's head whipped around, but Anna-Lisa stopped him with a hand on his elbow. "Outside," she mouthed, and got up.

As he walked past the sink, Marlow plunged his hand into the water and loosened the plug. The water gurgled down the drain and the little boat spun in circles. Anna-Lisa took Marlow's arm and led him into the hallway outside.

"I wanted to say," she whispered. "I think it's time you talked to him."

"About what?" said Marlow.

"About… you know. The facts of life."

"You're his mother," said Marlow, and realized how apalling that sounded.

"And you're a man," said Anna-Lisa.

Marlow's face reddened. "Is it really necessary? It's not as though he can get into any trouble—"

"Marlow, he needs to know these things," said Anna-Lisa. "Do this for me. Please?"

"All right. But not now. Later."

As it happened, Marlow's talk with Midway had to be postponed indefinitely. That night, Marlow was woken from a troubled sleep by a noise downstairs. As he lifted his head from his pillow, he heard it again. A sharp report, like a capgun firing. He shuffled into his slippers and turned on the hall light. The pop came again, this time like a hailstone landing on a plate. Halfway downstairs, Marlow caught a whiff of smoke. He stopped and sniffed again. No, he wasn't imagining it. He charged downstairs and immediately found the source of the smell. In the dining room, the buffet was on fire. Marlow snatched up a handful of magazines from the den and proceeded to bat the flames with them. When that proved futile, he made for the kitchen. He took two steps when his foot leapt out from under him and he crashed flat on his back on the hardwood floor. What looked like a ball bearing drooled loudly across the boards. Marlow picked himself up and bolted into the kitchen. He dumped out the fruit bowl and filled it with water then ran back to empty it over the buffet before he finally convinced the flames not to set up house there.

Examining the mess, he discovered an overturned candlestick, its wick still warm. He coughed and was answered with another sharp pop. Something struck his tailbone and ricocheted.

"Woops, sorry Uncle," said Midway. "Meant to hit the fondu pot."

Marlow turned around. The Teasewater case was open on the dining table. Standing amidst what looked like a pile of ball bearings were Midway and the Peeper. Midway, dressed in his best white linen suit, was holding an oar from his boat and… Marlow leaned closer. Between his lips was a thin taper from which a tiny tendril of smoke was curling.

"What the hell do you think you're doing?" Using his finger and thumbnail, Marlow plucked the smoking thing from between Midway's teeth. He sniffed at it. Cigar smoke. His eyes lit on the case of his best cigars which sat in pride of place in the middle of the table. The box had been opened and one of his cigars protruded over the rim. It had been eviscerated.

"You're *smoking*?" said Marlow. "*My* cigars?" He didn't know which was worse.

"The Otter's got a pipe," said Midway. "If he can smoke, why can't I?"

"Because it'll stunt your gr…" Marlow stuttered, at a loss.

"Gosh, and here's me hoping to crack six inches by my second birthday. Thanks, Uncle Marlow. That was a close one. Sorry about the fire, but, you know, I had a job lighting it from the candlestick and it sort of… fell over." Midway's facade of contrition disintegrated as he burst out laughing. Beside him, the Peeper slapped him on the shin warningly.

"And what's this mess here?" said Marlow, grabbing a handful of the ball bearings. He recognized them as a string of silver plastic beads used to garland the Christmas tree. He realized belatedly that someone had cut the end of the string. As he lifted them, they slipped off the string and bounced onto the floor.

"I was teaching him to play cricket," said the Peeper.

"If you'd stop throwing me googlies—"

"Oooo! That's very leg-before-wicket, Mr. Evans," said the Peeper, winking and shoving him playfully.

"Here, I'll show you how I'd hit one properly." Midway picked up one of the beads, tossed it in the air and winding up, gave it a whack with the plastic oar. The bead richocheted off the buffet table, hit the wooden floor and bounced.

"Marlow?" Anna-Lisa called from the doorway.

"Mind where you step," said Marlow. "Your son's dropped ball bearings all over the floor. And he's almost burned the house down."

"Midway?" said Anna-Lisa. "Are you all right?"

"I thought we'd agreed that nighttime was bedtime," said Marlow sharply. "I'm too tired to deal with this. He's all yours." Marlow splashed through the water on the floor and went up to bed.

After the cricket incident, Marlow drew up a set of house rules which Midway promptly broke. Anna-Lisa forgave him every transgression. By definition, he could do no wrong. Anna-Lisa refused to de-animate the animals or to separate them from Midway, thinking it cruel to deprive him of his friends. Marlow had other ideas. One afternoon while Anna-Lisa took Midway out in the back garden to show him the world outside, Marlow took the Peeper out of the case and brought him down to the workshop.

"What are you doing?" the Peeper demanded.

"You're a bad seed," said Marlow. Really, of all the Teasewater animals, he was the worst influence on Midway. He shut the Peeper off and began making painstaking alterations. He knew he didn't have much time. Anna-Lisa would be bringing Midway inside soon enough, and he would demand to know where his companion had gone. It was not a simple matter to change the Peeper's attitude to one of rigid obedience. It involved identifying the twisted energy that must have leaked out of him and into the Peeper in the first place.

Marlow had never had to undo any of his work before. It was a blow to his pride. Sounds overhead distracted him and guilt made him twitchy. In the end, he was not sure whether he had succeeded or not. When he reanimated the Peeper, it immediately sat up and leapt out of his hand. The next thing he knew, it had hopped behind a wall cabinet. And that was the last he saw of it.

T he Otter perched on the edge of the sink beside Midway. Both of them paddled their feet in the water. Midway clutched a fishing pole. "Uncle Marlow, chuck in a couple of minnows for us, would you?"

Marlow remained seated. He tipped himself another glass of whiskey. It was two days since the Peeper's disappearance and no one had said a word about it, other than Anna-Lisa, who'd been quite upset. Midway was as depraved as he'd ever been, perhaps moreso. And the Otter was beginning to fall under his influence. The worst seed of the Teasewater Five wasn't the Peeper at all, Marlow realized. It was Midway.

Marlow had to work up the nerve to even consider his next move. Altering the animals was one thing. But Midway was more than an animal. And yet, so much worse…

Marlow took another swallow. He only drank when he was losing his nerve; drunkenness gave him an excuse to dither.

"Marlow, you shouldn't do that in front of Midway," said Anna-Lisa, coming into the kitchen. "You're setting a bad example."

"Fine," said Marlow and he drained his glass and left it sitting on the table. He slunk upstairs. *Tomorrow,* he thought. *I'll deal with him tomorrow.*

Tomorrow came a bit late for Marlow. It was just past noon when he finally emerged from a coma-like sleep. He splashed himself to wakefulness under the bathroom taps before he remembered what he had planned to do today. *Midway.*

He shuffled downstairs, taking each step carefully. He comforted himself that he could do nothing while his head ached and his hands trembled. Downstairs in the kitchen, he found his whiskey glass still on the table. Upside down inside it was the Teasewater Vole. Marlow tipped him out onto the table. He wobbled a little, shook himself and hiccuped. He was wearing the vicar's costume, Anna-Lisa had made him. Marlow noticed that the table was covered with a sprinkling of what looked like dried parsley flakes.

"What the hell…?" Marlow said.

"We didn't have any proper confetti," said the Vole. "So we improvised. But I don't suppose that affects things."

Marlow noticed that the Teasewater case gaped emptily on the counter. "Where's Midway?"

"On his honeymoon," said the Vole. "I married them last night."

"On his *what*?! Married to whom?"

"The Bunting," said the Vole.

"But he's…" Marlow spluttered. "He's not even a mammal!" Then heard what he'd just said. "Where is he?"

"There's no point in looking for them. They've gone. After what happened to the Peeper, I can't say I blame them."

Marlow fumbled a bit with his hands; they seemed to be working independently of his brain. He scooped up the Vole and put him back into the whiskey glass and paced back and forth in the hallway. There was a breeze blowing through it. He followed it and found the French doors wide open on the garden.

Anna-Lisa searched for Midway for days, even sifting through the earth in the garden and in amongst the plants. Each morning she stood on the patio and called for them; the French doors were always left open now and Marlow spent sleepless nights envisaging thieves strolling in and looting the house. He had an alarm system and locks installed on his workshop. He felt no regret over Midway's disappearance, only shameful relief. Though it was hard to see Anna-Lisa suffer, he told himself it was for the best, and at least he had had no hand in it and therefore bore no blame.

Eventually, Anna-Lisa's searching came to an end. She cried for two days running and on the morning of the third, she buried the Teasewater case (with the Vole and the Otter inside) in the back garden next to the sun dial.

"One coffin, five bodies," she said. "Six, really."

Marlow turned over the last spadeful of earth and said nothing. There was nothing to say. And that was the end of the Teasewater Five, although some nights when he was trying to sleep, Marlow thought he heard peeping coming from inside the walls of his bedroom.

A week later, Marlow found Anna-Lisa eating at the breakfast table. Beside her plate lay a life-sized hand, long-fingered, with bitten-down fingernails. Golden hairs glazed the back of it where Anna-Lisa stroked it. She looked up and seemed to see Marlow then. She smiled. "It's a good start, don't you think?"